"You're not diving because I say so."

Luke's voice was perfectly calm. "And I'm the boss."

"That's not fair!" Melanie burst out. "I'm a fully qualified diver."

"On your last working dive, there was an accident," Luke said quietly. "A man died." He raised a hand to forestall her. "I know you were cleared of any blame."

"Then why—"

"The day before the accident, the night before, something else happened, something that's still haunting you?"

Melanie felt the color drain from her face. "I-I don't know what you mean," she whispered.

"Melanie, trust me."

She wanted to, so much. Her heart longed for his love, and her body quivered and sang at his touch. But her mind was locked in the memory of that terrible night....

DANA JAMES lives with her husband and three children in a converted barn on the edge of a Cornish village. She has written thriller, historical romance and doctor-nurse romances but is now concentrating her efforts on writing contemporary romance fiction. In addition to extensive researching, which she adores, the author tries to write four hours every day.

Books by Dana James

HARLEQUIN ROMANCE
2632—DESERT FLOWER

The Marati Legacy
Legacy
Dana James

Harlequin Books

TORONTO • NEW YORK • LONDON
AMSTERDAM • PARIS • SYDNEY • HAMBURG
STOCKHOLM • ATHENS • TOKYO • MILAN

Original hardcover edition published in 1986
by Mills & Boon Limited

ISBN 0-373-02841-5

Harlequin Romance first edition June 1987

My sincere and grateful thanks to Mr. Garry
Williams and Mr. Joe Revill, without whose
expert knowledge and generous assistance
this book could not have been written.

Printed in U.S.A.

CHAPTER ONE

LIKE a molten gold ribbon in the afternoon sunlight, the waterfall cascaded from the escarpment in spectacular leaps and vanished amid the lush tropical vegetation that fringed the bay. But Melanie had no eyes for the exotic scenery.

A frown creased her forehead and she was scarcely aware of the warm breeze teasing her long honey-gold hair and moulding the pale green crinkle-cotton of her skirt and blouse to her slender body.

Her sandals swung carelessly from one hand as she walked slowly along the ocean's edge. Yellow sand, still dark and damp from the afternoon downpour, crunched between her toes as she stepped into the limpid water. The warm ripples licked her feet and she tried to throw off the tension that had been her constant companion for so many months.

Behind her, the bright houses of Fort Dauphin were scattered like gaudy beads against the green hillside. The two-storeyed buildings with their steeply pitched roofs reflected a French heritage, though this strange, unique island of Madagascar was less than three hundred miles from the coast of Africa.

Melanie turned her back on the ancient town and stared out to sea. In the bay the water was a sheet of turquoise, barely ruffled by the breeze. But beyond the surf which marked the coral reef, a long swell surged ceaselessly towards the island, driven from the vastness of the Indian Ocean by the south-east trades.

The sea. It was her life. It had given her so much—hours of endless pleasure and a job she adored. She had always respected the sea, alert to its changing moods and to the elemental forces that within minutes could transform sapphire smoothness into a raging maelstrom of black water and white spume.

She had loved it, dedicated herself to it. But it had exacted a cruel price—first her grandparents, in a sailing accident, and then, almost four months ago, Paul.

What was she doing here? The question was born of despair. Why had she come?

'Mel! Hey, Mel!'

The sound of her brother's voice brought Melanie's head round. Her brown eyes narrowed against the sun's low rays and she raised one slim hand to push her hair from her eyes.

The sight of his familiar figure loping towards her across the rapidly drying sand, clad, as always, in T-shirt and faded jeans, took the edge off her doubts.

'Hi!' She waved wildly and ran towards him, dropping her sandals and laughing breathlessly as he swung her into his arms and whirled her around before setting her down again on the beach. 'Oh, Derek, it's so good to see you again!' She hung back, clasping his wrists, drinking in the tousled, sun-bleached hair, the brown eyes, high cheekbones and wide mouth. All—though harder, less delicately moulded—so like her own.

Her gaze flicked over his lean, rangy body which radiated health and energy and topped her five and a half feet by a good four inches. 'You're looking marvellous.'

His welcoming grin faded as he studied her. 'I wish I could say the same about you.' He shook his head. 'You're skinny, Mel. How long is it since you ate a decent meal?'

She winced but recovered at once. 'We haven't seen each other for two years and you're nagging already!' Her smile was almost normal. 'What about a little respect for your elder sister?'

Derek scooped up her sandals and, slipping an arm around her shoulders, began walking her back towards the hotel. 'Melanie, you have taken advantage of the ten minutes that separated our births for as long as I can remember. But it won't wash this time.' He squeezed her shoulder gently. 'You're not ill, are you?'

'Of course not.' Her denial was vehement. 'I'm fine. OK, so I've lost a little weight, but I've been working hard.' She flashed him a bright smile. 'If you could see the food we get at the Institute—cordon bleu it is not!'

'Have you seen a doctor? Hell, you *are* a doctor. Why haven't you done something about it?'

'About what? I've lost a little weight, that's all. What should I do? Reach for the pill bottle? No,' she said firmly, 'I'm handling it my own way. I'm——'

'Starving yourself? Working yourself into exhaustion?' Derek's tone was dry but not unkind. He pulled her round to face him. 'Mel, it wasn't your fault. Paul's death was an accident.'

'How do you know?' Melanie's face crumpled in anguish. 'You weren't there. You didn't see what happened.'

'Dick Benton wrote me after the inquiry.'

'He had no right——'

'Mel, he had every right. I'm your next of kin. Dick Benton is Director of the Institute. He's not only your employer, he's been a good friend to both of us. He was worried about you. Even after the inquiry confirmed that it was an accident, you were still insisting you were to blame. Then you became a workaholic, demanding to complete the programme of experiments you and Paul had been working on. You can't do oceanographic research under that kind of strain. You were becoming a danger to yourself and to the rest of the team.'

She stared at him. 'Is that why you sent for me? Because Dick Benton said I needed a break? Did you arrange this whole thing between you? Isn't there a job here for me at all? Was it all a lie?' The questions sprayed from her pale lips like bullets.

'Hey,' Derek shook her lightly, 'take it easy! I'm on your side, remember?' He tightened his arm around her and they started walking again.

Melanie kept her head down, not wanting her brother to see the tears that scalded her eyes yet refused to fall, refused to allow her their healing release. She was still so sure that she was right and they were wrong. It *had* been her fault.

'Mel, about the job——'

She glanced at him then half turned her face to the sea so that the warm breeze would dry her eyes and restore some colour to her cheeks. 'Is there a job, then? You didn't get me out here under false pretences?'

'No, I didn't,' he affirmed, smiling. 'It's a damn good job, as a matter of fact, perfect for you. Someone with medical training needed to assist with testing some new diving equipment.'

'You told me that much in your letter,' Melanie pointed out. 'But why did you ask me?'

'Why not?' Derek lifted one shoulder. 'You're medically qualified——'

'Yes,' Melanie interrupted, 'but I never practised medicine. I went straight into research, you know that.'

'Exactly. Research into the effects of pressurised gases under water. And you're a qualified diver. So, who better? Besides,' Derek pressed her shoulder again, 'it's worked out so well. The job coming up, Dick wanting you out of the Institute for a while, and you needing a break, but not a lie-around-and-do-nothing-but-brood type of holiday. Several weeks in the Indian Ocean with sun, sea, good food and a challenge is just what the doctor would have ordered,' he grinned.

Melanie gave him an old-fashioned look. 'When do I

meet whoever's in charge, and what will you be doing?'

'I'm supposed to be making a film record of the dives and the equipment in use. Actually I'm combining this job with a series of photo-articles on marine life around the coral reefs for *Wildlife* magazine. I reckon I'm in with a chance for the award this year.'

'Derek, that's wonderful!' Melanie hugged him. 'You always were my favourite underwater photographer——' she grinned impishly, 'after Jacques Cousteau, and Krov Menuhin, and——'

'I've heard they're quite good,' he cut in airily. 'But of course I'm too young to remember their work. Having an older sister is so useful.'

Melanie wrinkled her nose at him and began to laugh, momentarily startled by the happy sound issuing from her own throat. It was such a long time since she had laughed. The bands of tension around her head and heart loosened. A great weight seemed to slip from her shoulders. She tossed her hair back and felt it lifted by the soft, clove-scented wind. 'You know what?' She smiled at her twin.

'No, what?'

'I think I'm quite glad I came after all.'

'Wow! How's that for a positive attitude?' Derek grinned, and ducked as she aimed a punch at him.

They were about fifty yards from the hotel whose gleaming white façade was tinted rose by the sun as it sank towards the forested hills. The building, of French Colonial style, had a broad verandah supported by slender columns and fronted by a waist-high balustrade from which wide, shallow steps swept down to a vivid green lawn. Clusters of tall palms cast gently waving shadows. Jasmine, citronella and hibiscus bordered the grass in showy profusion, and beside the verandah a stunted tree bowed beneath the weight of fragrant yellow blossoms.

As Melanie gazed idly at the hotel, admiring its design and proportions, a tall figure wearing denims and a sleeveless black T-shirt came out of the hotel's main entrance. Leaning on the balustrade, the man surveyed the beach as though he were looking for something. As he caught sight of Derek and herself, Melanie saw him grow very still. He slowly straightened up, then swung himself off the verandah and started towards them.

Without knowing why, Melanie was suddenly apprehensive. 'Derek, someone's coming. Do you know him?'

'Mmm?' Derek had been watching a rust-streaked freighter chugging across the bay towards the entrance to the lagoon. He swung round. As he saw the man a muffled curse escaped his lips.

'What's wrong?' Melanie's tone was sharp though she kept her voice low. The tension was back, a clenched fist in her stomach, a tightening of the muscles at the back of her neck. It wasn't simply Derek's reaction, there was something about the approaching stranger, whose long, powerful strides made light of the yielding sand, that disturbed her.

'I didn't expect—I thought we'd have more time,' Derek muttered. His voice grew urgent. 'Listen, Mel, about the job——' Then he stopped, for the man was less than ten feet away.

The stranger stood over six feet tall. His black hair, though threaded with silver at the temples, was thick and as glossy as a wet seal. It curled untidily on his neck. The sleeveless T-shirt, patched with damp, revealed arms and shoulders corded with muscle and sheened with sweat. His skin was the colour of teak. Piercing blue eyes beneath straight black brows swept briefly over Melanie and she sensed herself appraised and discarded as of no importance. The slightly hooked nose was white around the nostrils and deep lines were scored on either side of a mouth whose chiselled lips were set in a thin line. The chin jutted, the jaw was hard and there was anger in every sinew of the lithe body.

'I was under the impression you came ashore to meet your brother.' The stranger's deep tones frosted the air as he fixed Derek with a glowering stare that sent a shiver down Melanie's spine.

'Luke,' Derek held up a placating hand, 'let me introduce you——'

'No.' The word was a whiplash and Melanie flinched. 'I have no wish to be involved in your private ... affairs.' The pause was brief but significant. 'Your social life is your own business, but not on *my* time.'

'Luke, hold it, I can explain——' Derek began.

'I'm not interested——'

'Oh, shut up!' Melanie blurted at the stranger, then blushed furiously. She hadn't even known she was going to speak until the words were out of her mouth.

Both men looked at her, Derek with sudden anxiety and the stranger with a surprise that bordered on arrogance.

Melanie dropped her arm from around Derek's waist and clasped her hands in front of her. Derek touched her arm in a warning gesture, but she ignored the pressure and glared up at the taller man. 'I don't know who you are, nor do I wish to,' her cool tones were belied by the whiteness of her knuckles, 'but I would like to know what gives you the right to talk to Derek in that manner——'

The man's expression had altered subtly. His features were still bleak, but the icy stare had been replaced by fleeting amusement and a more lingering speculation. 'I'll tell you,' he broke in, and some quality in his voice prevented Melanie uttering the retort that sprang to her lips at his interruption. 'I hired Derek to do a job. It's an important, rather complex business for which he's being paid extremely well. For his part, certain equipment he operates has to be ready for use as and when I need it. To ensure that it is, he needs spares, and it was partly for those and partly, so he told me, to meet his brother who will also be working on this project, that he came ashore.'

Melanie's mind was whirling. 'Just a minute.' She raised a hand as if to physically stem the brisk flow of words, perplexity creasing her forehead. 'I—I'm sorry, I don't understand.' She turned to her brother. 'Derek, what's he talking about? What brother?'

'Mel, I'm sorry,' Derek grimaced and shrugged awkwardly, 'I planned to tell you earlier. I did try, but there wasn't time.'

'Mel?' the stranger said, looking sharply at Derek and then at Melanie, bewilderment softening the harsh set of his features.

'Tell me what?' Melanie demanded. 'For heaven's sake, Derek, what's going on?'

'Driscoll,' there was a note of warning in the other man's voice, 'if you've done what I think you've done——'

Derek backed off a couple of paces and thrust his thumbs into the waistband of his jeans, affecting nonchalance. 'Luke, I never once used the word "brother". What I actually said was that I was going to meet my twin, and that Mel was the answer to our problem.'

'But you told me your twin was a doctor and a qualified diver.'

Melanie noticed that he didn't once glance in her direction, speaking of her as if she wasn't even there.

'That's perfectly true, I did, and so she is,' grinned Derek. 'Luke Avery, meet Dr Melanie Driscoll, my twin sister, at present on loan from the Oceanographic Research Institute.'

Disbelief clouded Luke's strong features as he and Melanie stared at one another.

As she realised this was the man for whom she was

supposed to be working, Melanie flushed deeply, recalling her first words to him. But her embarrassment was swiftly followed by indignation. She had nothing to apologise for. His appalling manners were surpassed only by his arrogance. Her expression must have revealed her thoughts, for Luke Avery's expression grew chilly.

'Well? Aren't you two going to shake hands? You know, like boxers before the first round?'

Derek's attempt at humour did nothing to ease the charged atmosphere, in fact his accurate reading of the situation provoked both Luke and Melanie to turn on him.

'Derek,' Luke's voice was tight with anger, 'of all the stupid——'

In the same instant Melanie, her eyes dark and hurt at her brother's trickery, said quietly, 'That was a rotten thing to do, Derek.'

'Damn it,' he cried in exasperation, 'what is it with you two? What's the problem? Luke, you've had non-stop hassles over the insurance conditions. Melanie has all the qualifications you need.' He turned to his sister. 'Everything I said to you a few minutes ago still stands. This job is exactly what you need right now and you could do it standing on your head. OK, I admit I didn't come right out and tell Luke you were female—he's got this bee in his bonnet about all-male crews—but I didn't lie. I just allowed him to think . . . I intended to set everything straight before you two met, but . . .' He spread his hands and shrugged.

'False pretences, Derek.' Melanie's words were barely audible. She shivered. The sun had disappeared behind the hills and purple dusk rolled down to envelop them. The heat of the day lingered in air as soft as silk and heady with the perfume of exotic flowers. But Melanie was chilled to her soul. She looked up at the tall figure of

Luke Avery.

'It appears we've both been misled. I'm sorry you've been inconvenienced, Mr Avery. If you'll excuse me?' She started forward, but her brother's arm shot out to stop her.

'Mel, I've said I'm sorry. Honestly, I didn't think you'd take it like this.'

She spun round her eyes blazing. 'Didn't you? Didn't you really? You didn't think at all, did you, Derek? Now let me pass, I'm going to pack.'

'Pack?' He looked shocked. 'What the hell for? You only arrived yesterday!'

'I have no reason to stay.' She tried to hold her voice level, but the familiar tightness was gripping her throat. She should not have come. She should never have allowed herself to be persuaded either by Dick Benton or by Derek. She had important work to do at the Institute; she should never have left it. Dick would understand that she had to come back. He couldn't really have meant it when he'd threatened to fire her if she didn't take at least two months off. He had her welfare at heart, she knew, but he hadn't understood. She needed her work. She needed the lab. New people and places were not for her; she needed the security of familiar faces and routines. She had been away a week already. They'd be missing her by now. She had planned the new experiments testing gas mixtures at different depths. Of course, they had all her notes, but she ought to be there in person to see it through, to make sure there were no more . . . accidents.

'Let me go, Derek.' She could hear the huskiness and swallowed hard. 'I have a lot to do.'

He released her arm and without a backward glance Melanie walked to the low wall that separated the beach from the lawn. She paused to pull on her sandals, then crossed the springy grass to the wide verandah steps, her back ramrod-straight, the lump in her throat threatening to choke her.

'Dr Driscoll!'

She flinched as Luke Avery's voice reached her. Reacting instinctively to its note of command, she faltered. Then she recalled his raking, dismissive glance, his refusal to even acknowledge her presence until absolutely forced to. She did not look round. Tilting her chin a fraction higher, she crossed the verandah and entered the hotel, conscious all the while of Luke Avery's piercing blue eyes boring into her back.

Slowly, Melanie replaced the receiver. Dick hadn't minded her phoning. He had not been able to disguise his surprise when she told him she was calling from Madagascar. He had been just about to leave the lab. Everyone was fine and the tests were progressing smoothly. She wasn't to worry about a thing, just enjoy her holiday, and his parting words, 'See you in seven weeks', made it perfectly clear that he would not accept her back one day sooner.

Luke Avery had made it obvious she wouldn't be working for him. Not that she had the slightest desire to have anything to do with so obnoxious a man. Now Dick Benton had slammed the only other door in her face. What was she to do?

A sharp rapping on the door made her jump. At once her misery and confusion found a focus. Derek. Had he telephoned Dick again? Spoken to him before she had had the chance? They had arranged this between them, blocking her only escape. It did not occur to Melanie that there was something not quite right about a young, attractive, single woman clinging to her work as an escape.

Getting up from the side of the large bed, anger welling inside her, she crossed the room and wrenched open the door. 'I hope you're satisfied, you've—Oh!'

Leaning against the jamb, arms loosely folded, Luke Avery raised a quizzical brow. 'Satisfied? It's a little too soon to say, don't you think? A knowledge of theory doesn't always make for practical expertise.'

Melanie tried to gather her scattered wits. This man was the last person she had expected to see. 'I—I'm—I thought you were——'

'Your brother. Yes, I know. May I come in?'

'Why?' Melanie tried to stand her ground, but Luke gently pushed the door wider.

'Because,' he said as she stepped back under the steady pressure, 'I'm not used to discussing business in hotel corridors.' He entered the room and closed the door behind him.

Melanie turned away. 'I wasn't aware we had any business to discuss, Mr Avery.' She went to the dressing table, anxious to put physical distance between herself and this man, yet not sure why. She opened her handbag and pretended to look for something.

'On the contrary. Oh, do stop fiddling with that. Come and sit down.'

Melanie's head jerked up. 'I *beg* your pardon?' Her anger, quashed by the shock of confronting him instead of her brother, began to bubble again.

To her surprise he dropped into the basket chair beside the french window and, leaning his elbows on his knees, raked both hands through his unruly hair, leaving it even more dishevelled. He raised his head and a wry smile transformed his face. 'Hell, I'm sorry. None of this is your fault. Your brother——' He broke off, shaking his head.

'Yes, well, what was it you wanted?' Melanie closed her bag with a decisive snap and moved it to a different position. Just being in the same room with this man made her unaccountably edgy. She couldn't think why.

She had worked with men since her student days, and they had always outnumbered women, especially in the lab. So why did Luke Avery unsettle her this way?

'I want you to stay on and do the job you came out here to do,' he said bluntly.

'No.' Melanie's response was instinctive and automatic.

He looked surprised. 'Why not?'

'I don't have to give you my reasons.'

'Yes, you do. You'd accepted the job. It was all arranged.'

'That was before.'

'Before what?'

'You know perfectly well.' Melanie was growing flustered, clasping and unclasping her hands. 'Before either of us realised my brother had made fools of us both.'

Luke stood up and went towards her. He was once more cool, urbane, and in control of the situation. 'Derek can only do that if we allow it. I admit I was surprised to learn that you were the twin he'd talked about. When he mentioned Mel being qualified both in medicine and diving, I naturally assumed——'

'Oh, naturally,' Melanie cut in tartly.

Luke's eyes narrowed. 'The pot calling the kettle black?'

She looked up quickly. 'What do you mean?'

'You're accusing me of chauvinism, and you're just as bad.'

'I am not!' she denied hotly. 'And I haven't accused you of anything.'

'Maybe not in words.' His mouth twisted briefly. 'But your eyes speak volumes.' His tone hardened, became inquisitorial. 'Are you good at your work?'

It was Melanie's turn to be startled. 'Yes.'

'Did you come out here with the clear intention of

working with your brother on an underwater project?'

Reluctantly she agreed, 'Yes, I did.'

'Derek told me you would definitely be available for two months, and that you had no reason to return to England before then. Is that right?'

Melanie couldn't deny it. 'Yes,' she muttered.

'Then you have no logical reason for turning this job down.' He was only an arm's length away. She was acutely aware of him, his man-smell, warm and musky, tinged with a faint tang of soap. His powerful presence filled the room. He was a man used to getting what he wanted. Yet there was no impatience in his manner, only an implacable determination.

'No *logical* reason,' he repeated softly, staring down at her. 'Of course, had I refused you just because you were a woman, that would have been sexual discrimination. No doubt you would have been angry. And quite rightly so.' His deep voice was quiet, hypnotic, and Melanie had to concentrate, to deliberately distance herself, listening only to the words, ignoring the resonance, the timbre, that played gentle fingers down her spine. He was turning all her arguments upside down before she'd even had the chance to put them.

'But I didn't refuse you,' he stated. 'I want you on the boat. Now give me one *logical* reason why you must leave.'

'Derek said you wanted an all-male crew.' She was clutching at straws, trying to hold out against the force of his personality.

One corner of his mouth lifted as if he were giving her a point for memory. 'What I actually said was that I usually work with an all-male crew—a situation dictated by circumstances rather than choice. I don't know of many female divers working off in-shore oil-rigs, where much of my work is done. As your brother has pointed out, you have the perfect qualifications for this project.

Why should I waste time and effort looking for a man?'

Melanie turned away. He'd won and they both knew it. She heard him walk to the door and turn the handle. 'I'll see you in the morning. Eight-thirty at the jetty.' The tone was polite, but it was an order nonetheless. There was a moment's silence and Melanie glanced up to see him watching her. His face was expressionless but she caught a glint of amusement in his gaze as he inclined his head. 'Goodnight, Dr Driscoll.'

'Goodnight, Mr Avery,' she managed, equally polite. He closed the door quietly behind him and Melanie sank down on the bed, wondering exactly what she had let herself in for.

CHAPTER TWO

MELANIE stared at the boat moored to the jetty and her doubts returned in force. She had woken that morning determined to make the best of what was, after all, a rare opportunity. She had never dived in tropical waters, never seen at first hand the rainbow-hued fish and brilliant corals in water as clear as glass.

Luke Avery had seemed so businesslike, so relentlessly efficient. Appearances were certainly deceptive!

Resembling an unhappy blend of small coaster and tug, the boat had a raffish, slovenly air about it. The superstructure, once white, was dirty, splattered with bird droppings and streaked with rust. Haphazard daubs of orange anti-fouling marked the scarred and weather-worn hull. A cracked and peeling nameplate fastened below the bridge identified the boat as *Painted Lady*. The corners of Melanie's mouth tilted wryly.

'A real old rust-bucket, isn't she?' Luke's deep voice behind her right shoulder made her jump. She spun round. 'Wouldn't you say she's the most disreputable old crate you've seen in years?' he persisted, his smile an odd mixture of pride and amusement.

Melanie shrugged helplessly. 'Since you ask, yes.'

'Good.'

Bemused by the obvious satisfaction her answer had given him, she watched him assess the vessel with a long, sweeping glance. Then he turned, subjecting her to the same scrutiny.

Not sure what she would be called upon to do that day, Melanie had dressed in pale blue cotton trousers, a matching short-sleeved shirt, and tennis shoes. Her hair was twisted into a neat bun high at the back of her head. Her only make-up was a touch of lipstick, applied solely to relieve her pallor and in the hope of deterring further comments from her brother.

'You've left your cases at Reception?' Luke took her arm and steered her towards the gangplank. His touch was warm, his fingers firm and strong on her bare skin. She nodded, and felt gooseflesh break out all over her body. A sudden, intense wish to be back in the anonymous safety of her hotel room gripped her.

'I'll have Herbie collect them later.'

'H—Herbie?' Her throat was dry and she had to clear it before her voice sounded normal.

'One of my crew. You'll meet them all in due course.' They stepped down on to the deck. To Melanie's surprise, despite the clutter of ropes, hawsers, buckets and other tackle, the deck planks themselves were scrubbed clean and bleached almost white in the sun. 'We'll go to the bridge first,' Luke announced. 'Follow me.'

Melanie's sharp intake of breath brought a hint of a smile to Luke's face as she stared around. Sunlight streamed in through Plexiglass windows; not one speck of dust or smear of oil marred the pristine surface of the banked consoles. 'That's a Decca navigator,' she pointed, 'and an echometer. This equipment is all brand new.'

Luke shook his head. 'Not all of it. But Callum keeps everything in good shape. Speak of the devil . . .'

A head tufted with thinning ginger frizz appeared through the hatch. Bushy eyebrows and a full beard covered the rest of the face, leaving only a bulbous nose and a pair of watery grey eyes visible. 'Ah've put new nozzles in the injectors. We'll no' have any more trouble.' The eyes swivelled from Luke to Melanie and back again. 'I dinna hold wi' lassies aboard.' The disapproving

voice issued from somewhere in the mass of facial hair,
but Melanie couldn't see a mouth at all.

'You're a superstitious old Jock, Callum Hendriks,'
Luke said calmly. 'Now come up here and meet Melanie
Driscoll, Derek's sister. She's a qualified doctor and
diver, and she's on the team.'

Callum heaved his bulk through the hatch with
surprising speed. 'Doctor, is it?' he muttered, wiping oil-
grained hands on a towelling rag pulled from a pocket in
his stained overalls. 'God save us, she looks like a
schoolgirl, and not an ounce of meat on her! Luke, are ye
out of your mind? She's no' right for this.' He glanced at
Melanie. 'No offence, lassie.'

'We've no choice, Callum. Time's running short, so
mind your manners.' Bland though Luke's tone was,
there was no mistaking the edge of authority. Melanie
wondered. He had not shown the slightest concern for
her feelings the previous day, so why bother now? Then
it dawned. Luke's concern was not for her feelings; he
was warning Callum not to say any more.

'Aye, well,' the engineer shrugged, 'it's no' my
business, but were I you, I'd tell Frenchie tae feed her up
a bit. Ah'm away below. Ye can test when ye've a mind
tae.' He disappeared through the hatch.

Melanie turned on Luke. 'Why do you all keep talking
about me as though I'm not here?' She was angry yet, at
the same time, she felt a strange urge to laugh.

'What do you mean, all? You've only met Callum——'

'You were the first,' she reminded him. 'When you
were talking to Derek, you refused to acknowledge my
existence.'

'That was before I knew who you were.'

'You wouldn't know now if I hadn't forced the issue.'
Seeing his face darken, Melanie decided to change the
subject. She had made her point. 'May I see the rest of the
boat?' He showed her, and the more she saw, the more

puzzled she became.

The tiny galley, all gleaming tiles and stainless steel, was immaculate. 'François, our cook, is ashore at the market,' Luke explained. 'This is Alain, his nephew and assistant.'

Alain, a lanky youth, with floppy, fair hair and a toothy grin, nodded shyly at Melanie and went on beating eggs in a metal bowl.

The air-conditioned saloon had a maroon carpet, oak table and leather chairs. Though a strongly masculine room, lacking any feminine touches, the overriding impression was one of comfort. It was a place to unwind and relax in. Melanie sensed that even in a blizzard in the Arctic, this room would be warm and inviting.

Luke led her down the passage. 'The first door leads to the showers; there are two. The second to the toilets.'

'Surely you mean the heads?' she corrected him sweetly. Confused she might be, and all too aware of her vulnerability in this totally male environment, but he didn't know that. Nor was he going to patronise her.

Luke glanced over his shoulder. 'You've dived from ships before, then?'

Melanie nodded. 'Several times, actually.' She didn't see that it was necessary to tell him those expeditions were day-trips out to diving locations, returning to the Research Institute each evening.

'Ah.'

Melanie tried to persuade herself there was far less significance in that word than she imagined.

'Then you'll be used to the accommodation.' He opened the first of two doors opposite those he had just indicated, and stood aside to let her pass. The room was a smaller version of the saloon. Richly carpeted, it contained a heavy, book-cluttered desk, a chart table spread with maps and diagrams, two maroon leather swivel chairs and a bookcase. Part of one wall was curtained off. 'This is my day cabin,' said Luke. Beyond the bookcase a door opened, and a middle-aged man in a white jacket and dark trousers appeared. 'Herbie, this is Dr Driscoll.' Luke turned to Melanie. 'Herbie is my steward. Anything you need, you simply ask him.'

'Good morning, Herbie.' Melanie smiled hesistantly.

'Good morning, miss.' Herbie's bow was a model of deference without servility. 'I have taken the liberty of unpacking your cases.'

Melanie's eyes widened as her gaze flew from the steward, past the open cabin door to the double bed, and back to Luke. His face was impassive, but she read amusement behind his level stare. She swung back to Herbie. 'There has been a mistake.' Her voice was flat.

'That will be all for now, Herbie,' said Luke as if she had not spoken.

'Now just a minute——' Melanie began furiously, but the steward had gone, closing the door softly behind him. Melanie glared at Luke, feeling her cheeks grow hot. 'All right, Mr Avery, let's get the position clear once and for all. I've agreed to work for you—that's all I have agreed to. So whatever else you may have had in mind, forget it.'

Luke tipped his head to one side, studying her as he would an unusual specimen of marine life. 'Dr Driscoll, I find people who jump to conclusions based on nothing but their own emotional hang-ups somewhat irritating.'

'How dare you!'

Luke was totally unmoved by her outburst. 'How dare I what?'

'You deliberately embarrass me in front of your steward. Then you have the effrontery to accuse me of jumping to conclusions when *my* clothes have just been unpacked in *your* cabin!'

Luke folded his arms. Melanie met his gaze defiantly, but the gritty blue eyes boring into hers sapped her confidence. 'Have I asked you to sleep with me?' he demanded.

She swallowed. 'N—not in so many words, no,' she admitted. 'But——'

'Believe me, Dr Driscoll, when I want to make love to a woman I don't need to resort to subterfuge or kidnapping. Mutual agreement is usually sufficient.'

Melanie flushed crimson. She'd done it again. In two strides Luke reached the curtain and whisked it aside to reveal a bunk, neatly made up with fresh sheets and blankets. A narrow shelf containing several paperbacks was attached to the bulkhead, and above that was an adjustable light.

'Have you forgotten, doctor? I was expecting Derek's *brother*. You will take the sleeping cabin, I shall use this. That was the planned arrangement. I see no reason to change it.'

Melanie could not just meekly accept without making certain there was no alternative. 'Isn't there another, separate cabin? Surely on a boat this size——'

'You're right,' Luke agreed calmly. 'There are two more cabins besides mine. Derek is in one, and the other has been rigged up as his darkroom. In the interests of speed, accuracy, and ... other considerations which need not concern you, Derek will be processing all the films himself. You can, if you insist, bunk in the crew's quarters. However, I have it on good authority that François snores, and Callum—well, you've already heard Callum's opinion of women on boats. I think you'd be well advised to stay right here.' His words had a ring of finality, and Melanie knew further argument was pointless.

The intercom above Luke's desk buzzed and he turned to answer it. 'Avery.'

Callum's voice, flat and metallic, filled the cabin. 'Will I test yon engine now?'

'Yes, Callum. But don't leave the bay—François and Derek are still ashore.'

'Aye.'

There was a click and Luke released the switch. He glanced at Melanie. 'I'm going to the bridge for a few minutes. When you've done whatever it is women do to make themselves at home, come to the diving room. It's at the end of the passage. The door is marked.'

Melanie hesitated before entering the sleeping cabin, trying to keep her anger burning. A colour scheme of cream and apricot, plus gleaming white paintwork, made the small cabin appear light, airy and far more spacious than it actually was. A thick carpet muffled her footsteps. Curtains at the porthole matched the Spanish bedcover. Beside the bed a unit held yet more books, the titles revealing a wide-ranging taste. *Whitaker's Almanack* rubbed covers with the latest Dick Francis. There were several biographies, a volume of philosophy and Larousse's *Geography of the World*. Diving manuals and books on archaeology and oceanography filled the lower shelf, while a compact cassette player and a container of about twenty tapes were held secure by a lip on the top shelf.

She felt like an intruder. This was Luke Avery's personal territory. She could smell the faint tang of his aftershave. Though he was physically absent, his personality still haunted the cabin.

Tentatively, she opened the built-in wardrobe. It gave her an odd feeling to see her dresses and skirts hanging beside Luke's shirts and trousers. Memories of Paul flooded her mind—Paul holding her, urging her to move in with him, laughing aside her doubts, nibbling her ear, telling her she was hopelessly old-fashioned, that virginity at her age was a positive social handicap. He had been so persuasive, and had sworn he loved her. He had never mentioned marriage, but then neither had she.

Nor had she sought it. Her career had come first. He had accused her of having too much ambition for a woman, said it wasn't feminine. But she didn't want to be a trailblazer, only to do her job well. She hadn't realised he saw her absorption as a rebuff, her attention to detail as a threat. There had been snide remarks, then quarrels. Now he was dead.

She shut the door quickly, then, with reluctance, pulled open the drawers of the chest. Herbie had allocated her the top two, while Luke had retained the bottom three.

There were fresh towels on the rail beneath the basin, and her toilet bag lay neatly on the shelf with her brush and comb. The air-conditioning hummed softly as she turned on the tap and ran cold water over her wrists, then bathed her flushed face. She didn't know what she had expected, but it certainly wasn't this. Drying herself, she looked round the cabin and recalled the rest of the boat. In his letter Derek had told her nothing about Luke Avery. Did he own this boat? Was it his permanent home? It certainly had every comfort and convenience. She stood quite still, the towel forgotten. If it was his, why, when no expense had been spared inside, did he permit the outside to look so run-down and shabby?

The faintest vibration transmitted itself through her feet. Stuffing the towel back on to the rail, Melanie hurried to the porthole and looked out. They were moving. Windows flashed in the morning sun as the town paraded past. The boat began to turn and she saw the fishing fleet clustered at the far end of the bay. Behind them was a vivid green band of forest and, beyond that, the smoky-blue hills.

The intercom's imperious summons startled her. She had wasted too much time. Smoothing a wayward tendril up into the honey-coloured bun, Melanie hurried down the passage towards the stern.

The range of diving equipment should not have surprised her. Money had been no object over the rest of the boat, and here was no exception. She walked slowly past shelves and bays containing masks, snorkels, torches, knives, fins and watches; gauges of various types, demand valves, slates and marker buoys. There were racks of air and mixed gas cylinders with harnesses hanging from hooks above, and deflated yellow lifejackets, looking like burst balloons.

She turned to examine a rail of wet and dry suits on hangers. Luke stepped out from behind it, making her jump. 'Do you creep about spying on everyone,' she demanded sharply, 'or am I just lucky?'

As he came forward, Melanie saw the tube of Neoprene adhesive in his hand. She bit her lip. He must have been bending down to mend a tear in one of the suits.

She looked down, clasping her hands to stop them shaking. 'I'm sorry,' she whispered, 'I shouldn't have said—you gave me a shock. I didn't know anyone was in here.'

Luke observed her for a long moment, his lips compressed. 'I think Callum's right,' he said eventually. 'You do need feeding up. I can't risk you diving in your present state.'

Melanie's head flew up. 'What do you mean?'

'Whatever's worrying you, Dr Driscoll, could endanger the rest of us.'

Melanie felt the blood drain from her face. 'No!' she blurted. 'No, it couldn't happen again. I wouldn't let it.' Her head was swimming. She could see Paul's glazed eyes and gaping mouth, the silver stream of air bubbles as he ripped off his mask. Behind her the door opened and her brother's cheerful voice filled the small room.

'Hi, you two. François might be an excellent cook, but he's lethal in that inflatable! We've been hurtling about all over the bay trying to catch up with this tub. God, has it been a morning! As well as a speed freak with no sense of direction, I've had to cope with——'

Melanie spun round, clutching at Derek. 'Tell him,' she pleaded. 'Tell him I tried to stop it. I aborted the dive, but Paul wouldn't listen. Tell him it couldn't happen again, Derek. Make him believe——' She glimpsed the shock on her brother's face before roaring darkness filled her head, her legs buckled and she slid from his grasp into oblivion.

Something cool touched her cheeks, then lay across her forehead. It was pleasant, soothing. She could smell rubber, salt water and talcum powder. The sharp aroma of adhesive hung in the air. She became aware of voices.

'Nitrogen narcosis.'

'Why didn't you tell me, for God's sake?'

'It happened months ago. I thought she'd be well over it by now. What on earth did you say to her?'

Luke ignored the question. 'Was she responsible?'

'For Paul's death? God, no! They really went to town on the inquiry—you know what safety committees are like. But she was completely exonerated. In fact, Dick Benton said she should have had a medal. She nearly lost her own life in that rescue.'

'Then why this? What's behind it? Were they close? More than colleagues?'

Melanie opened her eyes. She was lying on the floor, a Neoprene jacket folded under her head. Luke Avery took his hand from her forehead. His face hovered above her own.

She struggled to sit up, avoiding Luke's helping hand. She saw the concern in his blue eyes fade, replaced by anger, and looked quickly away. 'I do apologise,' she murmured huskily. 'I guess I'm not immune to jet-lag after all.' She got to her feet. 'I should have eaten more breakfast. I'm not used to the heat yet.' Her voice was stronger and as she looked up after straightening her shirt and brushing non-existent dust from her trousers, her head was clear and she could feel warmth returning to her cheeks. In fact, they began to burn as she realised what ammunition she had just handed Luke Avery. How could she expect him to treat her as he would a man if she fainted at his feet? She was filled with self-disgust. How could she have lost control like that? She had handled it so well up to now.

Usually she could tell when the pressure was building up, when the guilt was too much to bear. Then, she contrived to be alone until, by sheer will-power, she could overcome it, reduce it to manageable proportions and carry on with her life and work. This time she had had no warning. It was Luke Avery. He unsettled her. Since the first moment she had seen him on the hotel verandah, she had been fighting the urge to run, to get as far away from him as possible. But why? It didn't make sense.

'You all right Mel?'

As she turned to reassure her brother, Luke caught her eye, his gaze so compelling she could not break away. She mustered all her conviction. I'm fine, honestly.' In that same instant, held captive by Luke's intent scrutiny, she experienced a flash of insight that shook her deeply. Luke Avery *knew*.

She dismissed the thought at once. It was ridiculous, he couldn't possibly know. No one could have told him. She hadn't said a word to Derek. No one else had been there to hear the raised voices or see the struggle. Melanie shivered. The bruises had been hidden by her clothes. The next day, when they had pulled her out of the water and stripped off her wetsuit, it was assumed the plum and purple marks had been caused in her attempt to rescue Paul. And Paul was dead.

Luke turned to Derek. 'Did you get the lenses?' Melanie felt her tension begin to ebb. She was tired, imagining things. He couldn't possibly know. She turned her attention to what was being said.

'No, that's what's taken me so long.' Derek shook his head in disgust. 'First I was told they'd be with the morning delivery, so I hung about until that arrived. Needless to say, they weren't. After six phone calls I discovered they were still in Tananarive. I used your name to pull a few discreet strings and Pierre's promised to send them down by road today. They'll definitely be here by this evening, but it's going to cost.'

'Can't be helped.' Luke was dismissive. 'We must get started tomorrow. I want this job finished as soon as possible. The risks are increasing every day.'

Derek eased one of the wetsuits off its hanger. 'If you don't need me for anything else, I want to take a test film. I'd like some shots of the inner edge of the reef. How long will Callum be cruising up and down the bay?'

As he spoke, the rumbling engines roared, then faded and stopped altogether. Running footsteps pounded the deck. Luke glanced out of the porthole. 'He's finished. We're alongside again and Billo is tying up. Take him with you, he can help with your tanks. You can use the inflatable, just check the fuel level. And make sure you take stills as well as cine. Those cameras must be one hundred per cent reliable—there'll be no second chances.'

'Got it.' Derek finished packing and with Luke's help carefully fitted two air cylinders into a harness, attached the valves and hoses, and gently laid the set in a second bag. 'Right, I'll see you both later. OK, Mel?' She nodded, and hefting the two bags he grinned and let himself out.

Besides wanting to steer Luke's attention away from any reminders of what had happened earlier, curiosity was stirring in Melanie. For a routine project involving tests of new diving equipment, Luke Avery was being extraordinarily cautious. Several times he had mentioned increasing risks and no second chances.

'Is anything wrong?' she ventured.

He was frowning as he looked at her, as though his mind was elsewhere. 'No more than usual on this type of assignment,' he said drily. Abruptly he became brisk. 'When did you have your last medical?'

'Two months ago.'

'And?'

'And what?'

Exasperation darkened Luke's features. 'Did you pass?'

'Of course.'

'How thorough was it? I'm not doubting your word,' he added before she could speak. 'There are very good reasons for asking.'

Melanie lifted one shoulder. 'It followed the usual pattern, physical and psychological tests.'

He was watching her closely. 'And you passed everything?'

'I've just told you so.' Melanie looked down. She hadn't meant her impatience to be so obvious.

'Have you dived since the accident?' Luke's question hung in the air.

'Naturally.'

'How soon after.'

Melanie moistened her dry lips. She could hear her heart thudding. 'Two days.'

'How deep?'

'Fifteen metres the first time and thirty the next. I used scuba tanks on both dives. During the following week I went below fifty metres, breathing helium and oxygen by hose to a hotwater suit. I didn't panic, Mr Avery. I haven't lost my nerve.'

His expression softened slightly. 'I'm not questioning your courage, Melanie.'

It was the first time he had used her name, and the sound of it startled her. Since their meeting he had been so cool and impersonal. Now, while part of her was absurdly pleased by the compliment he had just paid her, the warning was loud and clear. She could not afford to become friendly with Luke Avery. Though she had tried to convince herself that the suspicion she had glimpsed in his eyes was simply a product of her overwrought imagination, she knew it was not. But only she and Paul had known the truth, and Paul was dead. The secret was hers alone. It cast a heavy shadow, but, as long as she had her work, she could accept the rest. She wished Luke would go away; surely there must be dozens of things demanding his attention.

'No doubt you're familiar with all this.' Luke's gesture encompassed the contents of the room. 'The boat also has a small recompression chamber aft of the engine room. There's direct access from a hatch on deck and another staircase through that door.' He pointed past the rail of suits.

Melanie nodded. 'Is there anything you want me to do?'

Her hopes were dashed as he shook his head. 'We're going ashore.'

'Where? Why?' She didn't want to go anywhere with him. 'Surely, if we're leaving in the morning——'

'That's precisely why we're going ashore now. Come on.' He opened the door and waited for her to precede him.

'Are we going to pick up supplies? Or spares?'

Luke shook his head.

'Then where are we going?'

'You'll see,' came the brief reply. 'François has packed lunch and I've hired a car from the hotel.'

'Yes, but——'

'Listen,' he cut in, 'once we start work the words "time

off" cease to exist. According to your brother, this trip
was supposed to be partly a holiday for you, so stop
fretting about all the things you think you ought to be
doing, and enjoy yourself.'

Oh, Derek, what have you done? Melanie murmured
silently. She followed Luke along the jetty. Faded jeans
hugged his lean hips and on his feet he wore expensive
but shabby training shoes. Beneath his short-sleeved
shirt the muscles in his bronzed arms bunched as he
swung the rucksack containing their lunch over his
shoulder. Melanie shivered.

Glancing round, he grinned at her. 'Stop looking like
that! This isn't a visit to the dentist. I promise you, you'll
be glad you came.'

Melanie attempted a smile. As he closed the door of
the Range Rover and walked round to climb into the
driver's seat, her unease was momentarily eclipsed by a
traitorous quiver of anticipation. She crushed it at once.
'Aren't any of the others coming with us?'

He eyed her thoughtfully and her cheeks grew pink.
Then he shook his head. 'Just you and I, Melanie.' He
started the engine and they swung out on to the dirt road.

CHAPTER THREE

THEY followed the road south for a while across a narrow, flat plain dotted with clumps of palms whose fan-like fronds reminded Melanie of peacocks' tails.

'Those are Ravenala palms,' said Luke, 'also known as the Traveller's Tree.' He slowed the car. 'You see those yellow flowers in that patch of scrub?'

'Those, you mean?' Melanie pointed. 'They look like ice-cream cones with a lid.'

'They're pitcher plants. They live on spiders and other insects. Some inquisitive fly falls in and the lid slams shut. It doesn't open again until digestion is complete.'

'Meat-eating plants?' she grimaced. 'I've always thought of flowers as decorative and sweet-smelling.'

Luke smiled. 'There are plenty of those in Madagascar. Did you notice that tree below the hotel verandah, the one with the tiny cream-yellow blossom?'

Melanie nodded. 'It's gorgeous. The scent used to fill my room at night. It's a little like jasmine, only sweeter.'

'It's called ylang-ylang. Mayotte, an island to the north-west, exports tons of it to France every year, for the perfume industry.'

She glanced sideways briefly. Luke was watching the road ahead, his expression bland and totally unrevealing. She turned to look out at the scenery, trying to think of something to say.

'Relax, Melanie,' Luke's voice was soft and he didn't take his eyes off the road. 'This is a fascinating place. There are things on this island that don't exist anywhere else in the world.'

There was a pause. 'Is that where we're going? To see

some of them?'

He nodded. He didn't appear to expect any comment and she didn't make one. All at once she was content to sit back and enjoy the view. Circumstances, fate, whatever one liked to call it, had put her here, and as Luke said, it was a short respite before the work that lay ahead. It was only as she relaxed against the seat that she realised how tense she had been.

A little further on they turned off the road and on to a rough track which climbed into the thickly forested hills. Low bushes, palms and prickly undergrowth gave way to rosewood, ebony and lofty tamarind trees. Lianas festooned the branches and hung in loops and curves like forgotten Christmas streamers, over dense thickets of giant ferns.

In places, sunlight pierced the canopy, spotlighting the waxy green leaves of a scarlet-berried bush, illuminating the brilliant orange, turquoise and velvety black wings of huge butterflies captured in its beam. Despite the engine noise, Melanie could hear the shrieks and whistles of birds, and caught the occasional flash of bright wings high above.

'It's fantastic, breathtaking,' she murmured. 'Couldn't we stop for a while?'

Luke glanced at her, a lazy smile deepening the creases at the sides of his mouth. 'No. Not until we reach our destination.'

'Where's that?' Melanie wasn't impatient, just intrigued. If Luke would not stop now, the place they were going had to be even more spectacular.

'Just this side of the Mandrare river.' He pulled the vehicle round a sharp double bend and slowed as they approached another. 'But before that, we——' He stamped on the brake; the abrupt, unexpected stop hurled Melanie forward, but Luke's arm shot out with incredible speed and caught her across the front of her shoulders, preventing her from hitting the windscreen.

The milling people on the path, their backs to the vehicle, were so absorbed in their singing and dancing, they hadn't noticed its approach.

'You OK?' Luke lowered his arm and changed gear.

Melanie nodded, breathing deeply as she fell back against the seat. 'What on earth are they doing?'

There were about twenty dark-skinned people in the group. Some of the men wore smock tops over loose trousers, others shirts and ragged shorts. All had wide-brimmed hats made of straw or palm leaf and several wore large white cloths draped around their shoulders.

The women's full-skirted dresses, made from cheap cotton print, were faded and patched. They too wore rough cloth shawls, one or two carried babies in them, the ends tied in front like a sling. The whole group were barefoot.

But Melanie's attention had been caught by two men carrying a pole beneath which was slung a long wooden box. The pole was being jolted backwards and forwards and swung from side to side.

Suddenly aware of the vehicle and its occupants, the group fell silent and backed away to the side of the track.

'Don't look at them,' ordered Luke.

Melanie turned to him, puzzled. But before she could ask why not, he added, 'It's for their sake, not yours—I'll explain later. Just keep looking straight ahead, pretend they aren't there.'

Totally bemused by this strange request, Melanie obeyed, though she was burning with curiosity.

As soon as they had passed the group Luke accelerated up the rough, rutted track and around another bend. Melanie saw him glance several times in the rear-view mirror. Resisting the urge to look back, she swivelled round to face him. 'Please, the suspense is killing me! What was all that about? What are they doing?'

Luke kept his eyes on the track as he wrestled the wheel round, trying to avoid the worst of the potholes. 'They're going to a *famadihana*, a re-burial ceremony.

Melanie stared at him. 'What do you mean, a *re-*burial? Surely people only get buried once?'

He shook his head. 'Not out here. The Malagasy have very strong traditions concerning the dead. Family ties are very powerful and they believe that everyone who dies should be buried in the family tomb. But because of certain rites which must be observed, the ceremony is pretty expensive. And, as burial must take place within two days of death, it's usually not possible to make all the arrangements and get together all the relatives, who might be scattered in different villages over a wide area, within that time. There are also other taboos which prevent immediate burial in the tomb.'

'What taboos?' Melanie had forgotten the heat, the rain-forest, and the discomfort of her sticky clothes.

'Well, the tomb can't be opened twice within a year, and children under five can only be buried in the tomb when it's opened for an adult. So the usual course is for the corpse to be placed in a temporary grave. Then, two or more years later, a suitable date, convenient to the whole family, is selected with the aid of an astrologer, and the *famadihana* takes place.'

'Why do they have to wait two years?'

Luke glanced at her. 'You're a doctor,' he said not unkindly. 'Why do you think?'

Melanie frowned. 'I don't understand.'

'Even in this climate it takes at least two years for flesh to decay from bones,' he said bluntly. 'That fact relates to the third taboo against immediate tomb burial, as anyone who dies of a contagious disease is forbidden burial in the tomb until their bones are clean.'

Melanie was appalled and fascinated. 'So that box, on the pole, contained——'

'A corpse,' he finished.

'But why were they shaking it about like that? And that singing, and all the frenzied dancing. It seems so—well, disrespectful.'

'It is,' Luke said. 'It's deliberate sacrilege. It forces the closest relatives to come to terms with the fact that the person they loved really is dead and separate from them, is nothing but a pile of dry bones. But when the party reaches the tomb the bones will be taken out of the box, rewrapped in colourful silk shrouds and treated with the utmost reverence. That part of the ceremony is a reminder that it's the dead who gave their descendants life. Most people, whether simple or sophisticated, are afraid of a dead body. These ceremonies, which force the husbands, wives or children of the deceased to handle the skeleton, help to overcome that fear. It's a sort of desensitising treatment.'

'What happens then?' asked Melanie. It was many months since her interest had been held by anything except her job.

Luke shrugged. 'Once the eulogy has been given, and a blessing by the local pastor, while the skeleton is cradled on the laps of female relatives, the bones are finally placed in the tomb and there's more singing and dancing.'

Melanie was quiet while she thought over all that he had told her. She braced herself automatically as the track wound around a steep hill, then began to slope down. 'Luke, why did you tell me not to look at them?' She spoke impulsively as she remembered his firm instruction. It wasn't until he turned his head, a strange light in his cool gaze, that she realised she had used his first name, thereby confirming his right to use hers, and moving their relationship on to a new, less formal footing. She was suddenly wary. That had been stupid, and careless. She could not afford to become friendly with Luke Avery. Unnerving and too perceptive, he was, in some way she could not quite grasp, a threat.

And yet, to her dismay, she was drawn to him. She had never met anyone whose knowledge and interests were so wide. He obviously knew a great deal about the island and its people and seemed happy to answer her questions. Hadn't he told her this trip had been organised for her benefit, because she was supposed to be on holiday? But was that the only reason? She didn't think so. His excuse about no time off once the job was under way sounded all right to begin with, but she'd lay odds that wasn't the sole purpose. He could simply have given her the day off to spend on the beach, or look around Fort Dauphin, or even go with Derek. But he had insisted she come with him and that they come alone. Why?

Her heart began to pound and her hands were cold. Tiny beads of perspiration dewed her throat and upper lip. She wiped her forearm across her forehead, feeling it damp. Stop it, she told herself firmly. There was nothing to fear. He was almost a stranger. It was friends who— she blocked the thought, thrusting it aside. Polite, pleasant but distant, that was how she would behave. She'd be safe then.

She felt Luke's eyes on her, sensed his penetrating gaze. Stretching her mouth into a smile, she tugged at the neck of her shirt. 'Muggy, isn't it?'

His eyes were full of irony as he switched his gaze back to the track. He did not reply.

Melanie swallowed. 'Well? Are you going to tell me why I wasn't supposed to look at them?'

'Do you really want to know?'

'I wouldn't have asked if I didn't,' she responded, her tartness due mainly to an uncanny feeling that he had somehow known what she was thinking, which, she told herself, was utterly ridiculous.

'We're *vazaha*,' he explained. 'The word means

anything to do with Europeans. But another interpretation is clever or crafty, a quality the Malagasy think is typical of Europeans, and which,' his tone grew dry, 'they fear rather than admire. As *vazaha* we're believed to be heart-thieves.'

'Heart-thieves?' Melanie repeated in astonishment. 'How? I mean, in what way?'

'Ninety per cent of the Malagasy work on the land as owner-farmers. This has been their way of life for generations. But none of the Europeans with whom they come into contact live like this, yet they possess not only power, but all kinds of very desirable goods, so the ordinary Malagasy feels cheated. From his point of view the foreigners must be having more than their share, and therefore depriving him of those things, but he can't work out how. It's only a very short step for the Malagasy to imagine the European stealing his very heart and life-blood.' Luke glanced at her and she nodded, anxious for him to go on.

'Because of the cult and taboos attached to death, fear of the supernatural, of witches and so on, is very real. Had we stopped, or even watched them, because we're *vazaha*, we would have caused a great deal of anxiety and unhappiness.'

'Do they feel the same about everyone? I mean, don't they make friends with any foreigners at all?'

He shrugged. 'Possibly, in the capital or Tamatave, the main port. But road and rail links aren't very good in Madagascar, and most of the people don't meet enough foreigners to overcome their instinctive mistrust. Traditionally, the only permanent relationships are made within their kinship group. Anyone who isn't a kinsman, that is related either by blood or marriage, is believed to be dangerous and a potential witch. In fact, Malagasy who work in cities in positions of authority, or who are seen to possess things like cameras or radios, are also viewed by their countrymen as heart-thieves.'

The track broadened as they drove past a clearing in which stood a group of reed-thatched huts. Each hut was raised a couple of feet from the ground on wooden stilts, and the walls and floor were braced with thick lengths of bamboo.

'Why are they built like that?' asked Melanie.

'Floods,' Luke said briefly. 'Though here on the eastern side of the island it's wet all the year round, there are specially heavy rains from December to July. Streams turn into rivers, rivers burst their banks, uprooting trees and washing away the soil. Flash floods are all too common and the effects can be devastating. A trickle can become a roaring torrent in seconds, sweeping away everything in its path.'

'But where is everyone?' Melanie peered out both sides. 'The place looks deserted.'

The people on the track probably came from here, and there may be others tending their land or animals, or away in another village or town.'

Luke drove on. Silence fell between them, but to Melanie's surprise it was not strained but easy, companionable. She suddenly realised there was no need for continuous talk, no urgency to fill the quiet with words. As she thought over all he had told her, it occurred to her that Luke had made no attempt either directly or indirectly to get her to talk about herself. He had answered her questions freely and fully, but had not initiated any conversation. Could she have been wrong? To be always on her guard, permanently suspicious, went against her nature. But a small voice warned, 'remember Paul'. If only she could put it all out of her mind and give her whole attention to the surroundings. But how? Luke Avery was part of the surroundings and, even in silence, his was a powerful, all-pervading presence.

The track was almost level now, and driving on to a

lay-by at one side of it, Luke drew the Range Rover to a
smooth stop and turned off the engine. 'We walk from
here,' he announced.

Melanie was glad to stretch her legs. Despite the air-
conditioning her shirt and trousers clung. Though in
honesty she had to admit it wasn't solely the heat that had
made her perspire. She breathed deeply, inhaling the
scent of damp earth and decaying vegetation.

Locking the doors, Luke swung the rucksack over his
shoulder, and gesturing for her to follow, set off across
the track. A path led off to the right, through a screen of
leafy bushes and ferns.

'What is this place?' Melanie directed the question at
Luke's broad back as she plodded after him, her sandals
sinking into the soft ground which smelled sickly sweet
and musty. Her foot hooked a fallen branch and she
stumbled. She grasped the nearest tree trunk to steady
herself, but recoiled at once as her hand landed on a
squirming cluster of caterpillars. Snatching her arm
back, she bumped against another tree and glanced
round to see what looked like a rough piece of bark by her
shoulder detach itself and slither upwards into the
foliage.

The shock made her gasp, and Luke, taking the
situation in at once, explained, 'Tree gecko. Amazing
camouflage, isn't it?'

'Oh, amazing,' she agreed through clenched teeth,
waiting for her heartbeat to return to normal. 'Will you
please tell me where we're going?'

He didn't reply. He appeared to be listening to
something else as he scanned the forest ahead.

Melanie felt a pang of irritation. 'Look, I'm getting
rather fed up with——' Luke swung round, a finger to his
lips, then taking her arm, he drew her forward to stand
beside him and pointed to their left.

Crouched in the fork of a tree about fifteen feet from

the ground sat an animal unlike any Melanie had ever seen. It was poised in the act of eating a fruit held daintily between its front feet. Two round yellow eyes stared down at them from a pointed black face. Its neat little ears and cap of black fur gave its head a triangular shape. The rest of its coat was a rich creamy-white to the tip of the long, fluffy tail curled over the branch.

'What is it?' whispered Melanie.

'A sifaka.'

The rustle of their whispers was enough to break the spell holding the animal immobile and, dropping the fruit, it swung away through the trees in great leaps, its long limbs scarcely seeming to touch the branches.

'What is a sifaka?' Melanie enquired as Luke started forward along the path once more. He was still holding her arm, and short of wrenching it free, an action which would surely arouse comment, not to mention drawing far too much attention to what she had to assume was merely a helping hand, she could only try to ignore the warm pressure of his fingers just above her elbow.

'A kind of lemur. There are twelve different species, all unique to Madagascar. Though they don't look like the others, they are actually primates.'

'Like monkeys?'

He nodded. 'But much lower down the evolutionary scale. Some are as small as mice, others can be up to four feet long. They're mostly nocturnal but, as you see, a few feed in daylight.'

'What do they eat?' Melanie was trying desperately to concentrate on what he was saying, to divorce herself from his touch and the fear that clenched her stomach in its icy fist.

'Fruit and berries, insects and small reptiles,' he replied, his eyes narrowing as he peered through the tangle of branches and vines.

Balanced on a twig, a muddy-brown chameleon with

orange patches on either side of its serrated spine shot out an immensely long tongue and snapped up a cricket.

A striped lizard with a long spiky tail darted across the path in front of them. High in the lofty canopy birds squawked and screamed. Moths and butterflies, some dull and plain, others painted with surrealist patterns in neon colours, danced silently through rays of sunlight. The forest teemed with life. Insects rustled and buzzed and even the rotting trunks of fallen trees supported slender bell-capped toadstools, plate-like fungi, tiny pink orchids and butter-yellow impatiens flowers.

Luke's fingers tightened on Melanie's arm, and she froze. Then she realised he was pointing at something. Just ahead, where the path entered a small clearing, a group of five lemurs were picking clusters of scarlet berries off a bush. They called to each other in rapid bursts of chatter as they moved about on elegant limbs, their long fluffy tails, the pale fur interspersed with rings of black, held straight up, like periscopes.

Luke leaned down to whisper in her ear. His nose brushed against her hair and his breath was warm on her cheek. His words didn't register as adrenalin flooded her bloodstream, charging her with nervous energy, poising her to fight or run. She began to tremble, and suddenly Luke stepped back, studying her, a deep frown scoring his forehead.

The sound and movement alerted the animals and squealing in alarm, they fled.

'What's the matter?' he demanded, letting go of her to catch the rucksack as it slipped from his shoulder.

Melanie wiped her forehead with the heel of her hand. A bead of perspiration trickled down between her breasts. 'I'm—I'm a bit dizzy.'

'I should have realised you aren't used to this heat,' he glanced at his watch, 'and it's a long time since breakfast,

and if I remember correctly, you didn't have much of
that.'

She lowered her eyes, so anxious to hide her relief that
she didn't see his jaw tighten or the glitter in his
narrowed eyes.

'Come on, it's not far to the river. We'll have our lunch
there.' He led the way along the path.

They finished their meal with fruit, and after licking
mango juice from her fingers, Melanie kicked off her
sandals. Rolling up her trouser legs, she stood up and
slithered down the sandy bank. She stepped into the
shallow channel of clear water that meandered down the
wide river bed and crouched to rinse her hands.

Glancing up, she saw Luke watching her. Supported
on one elbow, his long legs stretched out in front of him,
he was idly trickling handfuls of fine yellow sand through
his fingers. His eyes were hooded against the sun's glare.

'The water's gorgeous, don't you want to bathe your
feet?' She really did feel much better now she'd eaten and
could almost convince herself that hunger, strain and the
heat of the sun had been the cause of her earlier distress.
During the meal Luke had asked her about the Institute,
and they had discussed the relative merits of working in
Bergen, where she was based, and in California where he
had done part of his training.

As usual, talking about work had relaxed her, and
without realising it she had grown confident and
vivacious. Absorbed in describing an experiment in
saturation diving when she had remained on the ocean
floor in a diving bell for fifteen days, Melanie had failed
to notice subtle changes in Luke's expression. She hadn't
realised his close attention had nothing to do with her
professional expertise, though he had not missed a word.

He shook his head. 'When you're ready I want to talk
to you.'

She stiffened. The wry curl of his mouth warned her he had noticed her reaction.

'It's to do with the job,' he added.

She waded out, scrambled up the bank and sat down about three feet away, leaning on one hand, her legs drawn up. Apprehension mounted inside her. 'What about the job?' she prompted.

'Ah yes, the job,' he repeated. He looked at the ground for a moment, seeming to search for words, then he raised his eyes to meet hers. 'Derek told you it involved testing some new diving equipment?'

'Yes,' Melanie nodded.

'Well, that's not strictly true. The equipment has already been tested. We're here to use it for a particular purpose. But it's vital that no one outside ourselves and the crew knows the real reason.'

'What is the real reason?'

'To recover part of a cargo from an East India Company ship which was wrecked on the coral reef north of Fort Dauphin over two hundred and fifty years ago.'

Melanie stared at him, uncomprehending. 'But why the secrecy? Wrecks are being excavated all the time— look at the *Mary Rose*.'

'There are several reasons,' Luke said quietly. 'The first is that salvage of wrecks is subject to some very stringent rules and regulations which, in this case, for reasons I'm not prepared to go into, have been short-circuited. Second, that particular ship should not have been carrying that cargo. Only a very few people know about it, and secrecy must be maintained. Which brings me to the third reason, and that is piracy.'

Melanie's eyes widened. 'What?'

'Oh, they still exist.' A wry grin twisted Luke's mouth, but his eyes remained serious. 'Only now instead of crimson shirts and a flashing blade, they operate as businessmen, complete with dark suits and briefcases.'

'This is a joke, isn't it?' But she couldn't summon a smile.

'No joke, Melanie, this is deadly serious. No one, and I mean no one, off the boat must have any idea of what we're doing. Our cover is good and fortunately close enough to the real purpose of our mission to satisfy any not-so-casual observer.'

'Are you expecting any?'

Luke shrugged. 'Precautions are never wasted.'

Melanie gazed across the river to the forested bank opposite, her thoughts racing. Things began to slot into place. The dilapidated appearance of the boat, for example. There were thousands that looked just like it, little tramps, plying between ports in all the oceans of the world, barely worth a second glance. No wonder Luke had smiled when she had agreed it was a disreputable old rust bucket! That was his protection, all part of the cover. Now she understood his insistence on all the equipment being in first class order, his anxiety over delay and his warning of no second chances.

Yet there he was, stretched out on the sand, appearing perfectly relaxed. Not once had he given the slightest hint of anything on his mind but their trip to see the lemurs. It suddenly occurred to her how much trust he was placing in her. A brief memory of Callum's ginger head swinging slowly from side to side as he told Luke she wasn't right kindled a fierce determination to prove the engineer wrong. She was equal to anything the mission might demand of her. Hadn't Luke himself said he didn't doubt her courage? 'Do you know exactly where the ship is lying?' She drew her knees up to her chin and hugged them.

'Not exactly, but I've a fair idea from records kept at the time plus computations of winds, tides and currents.'

Puzzlement drew her brows together. 'What records?

The ship's log couldn't have been saved, otherwise surely the rest of the cargo would have been recovered as well?'

Luke regarded her thoughtfully. 'I knew I was right about you,' was his enigmatic reply.

Melanie looked away quickly, uncertain.

He went on. 'The records were kept by a man with excellent reasons for knowing most of the ships using the Middle Passage between Mauritius and Madagascar on their voyage from India home to England. He spent part of his working life near Tamatave on the east coast, and the rest on the island of St Mary, nine miles off the mainland.'

'Who was he?'

'The leader of the Marati, the most vicious band of pirates ever seen in the Indian Ocean. He was an Englishman, and his grandfather, John, had been known as "The King" and from 1665 to 1705 had virtually controlled all Malagasy ports.'

'Yes, but what was his name?'

'His name? Oh, yes.' Luke sat up, dusting off his hands, then rose easily to his feet. He scooped up the rucksack and slung it over his shoulder. 'His name was Lucas Avery.'

Melanie's head snapped up. 'But that's—I mean, you're——'

'Yes,' he said drily. 'Come on, we'd better be getting back, it will rain soon. We get a downpour almost every afternoon.'

Hurriedly brushing the sand off her feet, Melanie put on her sandals and quickly rolled down her trousers. She didn't know what to think or what to say. How did you ask a man you'd only known a day if the name was simply coincidence, or whether he was in fact a descendant of the leader of a notorious gang of brigands? It would hardly be tactful. And hadn't he avoided asking her any personal questions? Had that been a deliberate move on his part to discourage curiosity from her? If she began to probe, then he would have every right to do the same, and that was something she wanted at all costs to avoid.

Melanie tried to concentrate on her surroundings as they made their way back through the forest. Luke showed her a shy, ruff-necked lemur, and a tenrec, which looked like a cross between a porcupine and an anteater. But her thoughts were drawn back repeatedly to what Luke had revealed as the true purpose of the job, and to the possible connection between himself and the Lucas Avery of two centuries earlier. How had Luke obtained the records? For whom was he retrieving the cargo?

She thrust the questions aside. Right now it was enough to come to terms with what would be required of *her* in this new situation.

During the ride back Luke spoke seldom, apparently sensing her need for time to adjust. He had said that all the crew knew. Which meant that not only was there a very strong bond between them if he trusted them that much, but that Derek too had been in on it all along. Yet he'd not given the slightest hint. His word to Luke had carried more weight than any loyalty to her. For a moment anger flared at his betrayal. He was her brother, her twin. How could he have kept something so important from her, especially as it was he who had persuaded her to come in the first place?

Gradually logic and common sense reasserted themselves. How could she expect Derek to break his promise? He had been sure she was right for the job, and in spite of their calamitous start, Luke Avery had taken her into his confidence, which showed that he concurred. He was placing a great trust in her, which demanded equal return. But how could she give that and retain the distance between them that was vital for her peace of mind?

The problem occupied her through her shower,

through dinner—she barely tasted the delicious seafood, hearing little of Derek's description of the reef—and into bed.

Lying between the crisp sheets, aware of Luke moving about in the day cabin, she tossed and turned. Being part of the team was going to demand a far greater commitment than she had ever imagined. She was used to having space around her, time alone. Such luxury was out of the question in the confines of the boat, with the ever-present threat of their cover being blown adding pressure to a task with its own dangers.

The emotional demands would be even greater. All her holds on security and self-protection were being systematically demolished by Luke Avery. She should be terrified, and when he touched her, she was. Yet despite all that, she could not pack and leave—partly because she had no legitimate reason and no place to go, partly because of professional pride, but partly because she was drawn, a moth to his flame. Would the growing warmth soothe and heal her scars? Or would she be engulfed and destroyed? She shifted restlessly. Her eyelids fluttered and closed and she fell into an uneasy sleep.

CHAPTER FOUR

WHEN Melanie woke the next morning and swung her legs out of bed the vibration of the cabin floor told her the boat was under way. Pulling back the curtains, she looked out of the porthole. It was a glorious morning. The sea sparkled turquoise and in the clear blue sky birds wheeled and soared. But the height of the sun warned her it was later than she thought. A glance at her watch made her gasp.

After splashing her face with cold water, she pulled on the clean shirt and trousers she had worn at dinner the previous evening. Raking the brush through her hair, she tied it back quickly into a ponytail. Then, hearing movements in the day cabin, she braced herself for a pointed remark about her tardiness, and opened the door.

'Morning, miss,' Herbie smiled as he looked up from tidying Luke's bunk.

'Oh—er—good morning, Herbie. Is Luke—Mr Avery at breakfast?'

'I doubt it, miss. He passed the galley over two hours ago. I wouldn't know what he's doing now.'

'Oh, I see. Do you know where I'm supposed to go? Did he leave any message?'

'Yes, miss, he said to tell you to be sure to eat properly this morning.'

'Thank you.' She gritted her teeth. It was pointless getting angry with the steward, he was only passing on what he'd been told to say. Besides, Melanie smiled ruefully as she left the cabin, it was plain where his loyalty lay. Though cheerful and polite he wouldn't even tell her where Luke was.

What was it about the man that inspired such allegiance? The crew had obviously worked together for some time, so a sense of comradeship was bound to have developed. But what about Derek? He hadn't known Luke long, yet he too seemed to have fallen under the spell of the man's personality. But why should she query it? She was beginning to recognise its force herself.

The saloon was empty, but as she looked around, François appeared from the galley. He was short and round. A crisp white apron covered his open-necked shirt and blue and white checked trousers, its strings tied in a neat bow over his paunch. His pale scalp was draped with strands of black hair lifted from a parting just above his left ear. In contrast to the sparseness on his head, his double chin, though recently shaved, was blue-black, and his walrus moustache the most luxuriant Melanie had ever seen. From under one side of it emerged a Gauloise cigarette, with half an inch of ash clinging precariously to the end, yet no tell-tale specks marred the snowy surface of shirt or apron.

'*Bonjour, ma p'tite*,' he greeted her, deftly setting a place at the long table and motioning her to a chair. '*Le capitaine* 'e say you need good food. Me, I prepaire ze best. You sit, I bring.' He bustled out, and Melanie couldn't decide whether to be amused or irritated. Just how many people had Luke informed of her dietary requirements? Almost against her will a smile curved her mouth as François reappeared, one eye screwed up against the smoke from his cigarette, which did not seem to have moved although the ash had gone. He set a bowl in front of her with a flourish. It was filled with chilled slices of pineapple, mango and guava. 'When you finish this, I 'ave ready ze fish.'

Melanie opened her mouth to protest. Other than the occasional bowl of porridge, she never ate a cooked

breakfast. But before a word could emerge, François
picked up the spoon and thrust it into her hand. 'No talk,
is good for you.' He leaned down slightly. 'You want to
dive, you eat, OK?' and without waiting for her reaction
he waddled out.

She stared after him. Was that too a message from
Luke? Or was François using his own methods of
persuasion? She shook her head and started her
breakfast. The cool, tangy fruit left her mouth delight-
fully fresh. Just as she finished, Alain sidled in, peeping
shyly at her from behind his floppy forelock. He too wore
a pristine apron that covered him from chin to knees.
Once more Melanie was reminded of the standards
demanded by Luke Avery, even over such apparently
minor details.

'Good morning, Alain,' she handed him the dish, 'that
was delicious, thank you.'

He coloured vividly and almost dropped the spoon.
'*Merci, m'selle.*'

'*Allez, vite!*' his uncle shooed him away with a jerk of
his head. Melanie smiled at the boy and he grinned back,
then loped out into the galley.

'I'll never manage all this!' she cried in dismay as
François set an oval plate in front of her. It was piled
with tiny fillets coated in golden-brown batter. Lemon
slices decorated each end of the plate.

'*Alors*, is not much. You will see, once you taste, you
eat them all. I make fresh coffee. *Bon appetit.*'

Perhaps it was the implied threat of not diving if she
didn't eat a good breakfast, but Melanie discovered an
appetite that surprised her. The contrast between the
thin, spicy batter, sharp lemon juice and sweet tender
fish was so mouthwatering that to her astonishment she
cleared the plate.

'*Bon.*' François nodded his satisfaction as he put down
a cup of steaming coffee and took her plate. A new

cigarette had replaced the old, and ash was beginning to form on its tip. Where did it go? How did he keep it out of the food? How long had it taken Luke to bow to the inevitable? 'When you finish your coffee you go.'

Compressing her lips to hide the smile François's bossiness provoked, Melanie had to admit she had thoroughly enjoyed the meal and felt very comfortable.

A few minutes later she entered the diving room. Clad in an orange and black wetsuit, Derek was sitting on a bench adjusting the waterproof casing on his camera.

'Hi,' she greeted him. 'Did the lenses arrive?'

He raised the camera. 'All safe and sound.' He grinned. 'How was your trip yesterday? I could hardly get a word out of you at dinner.'

'Interesting,' Melanie's tone was wry, 'and I'm not just talking about the lemurs either. Derek, what's the full story?'

'Full story? What are you talking about?' He looked puzzled.

'Come off it.' Melanie sat down beside him. 'What exactly is this cargo we're supposed to be salvaging? And who is behind the operation? Who is Luke doing it for?'

Derek stood up and lifted the harness on to his shoulders, moving the straps to settle the cylinders more comfortably. 'How should I know? It's not my problem. I'm only here to take pictures, and believe me, that's quite enough to worry about. I'm certainly not looking for anything else to fret over. If you want to know, why don't you ask Luke? By the way, I think he wants you up on deck.' He grinned and turned away to pick up his weight belt. 'Not so bad once you get to know him, is he?'

'I'm reserving my judgment,' Melanie retorted, but walked out before her brother could notice and question the flush in her cheeks.

Up on deck the air was crystal clear and a warm breeze ruffled over her skin like silk. In the clear deckspace at the stern she saw Luke. He had his back to her and was studying the coastline with binoculars.

They were some distance from the shore and travelling parallel with it. Melanie could see no signs of human habitation. There was just a narrow strip of grassland dotted with palms between the beach and the craggy, forested mountains.

Twice, Luke lowered the binoculars to refer to a notebook stuffed into the back pocket of his jeans. Then he scanned the coastline, gradually turning until he was almost facing her.

She felt a moment's awkwardness. Everyone else had obviously been up for hours. Why hadn't someone called her? She was here to work. She wanted the same treatment as everyone else. Was Luke waiting for an apology?

'Morning,' he said briefly, and without lowering the glasses he made another slow sweep of the shore.

Melanie was about to reply when the engine note changed, swelling from a deep, steady rumble to a roar. The boat slowed its forward movement, then stopped as the propeller went into reverse. Up on the bridge Callum opened the door, gave a thumbs-up sign and shouted 'Twenty', then disappeared again.

'What's happening?' asked Melanie. 'Have you found the wreck?'

Luke placed the binoculars gently on the deck and picking up a sextant peered through the eyepiece towards a tall palm at the edge of the beach. He made a note in the book. 'According to the Decca, something is down there, and it ties in with where we think it should be.' He turned away and took another sighting. 'But I want to see for myself. It's highly unlikely we'd hit it first time.'

'Then why are you wasting time?' The question just popped out. She hadn't intended to actually say it.

Luke made another note in the book, then pushed it

back into his pocket. 'I never waste time,' he said quietly. Melanie looked down. '*If* this is the wreck, and *if* the Decca equipment goes on the blink, how are we going to find it again without an accurate fix? That's what the sightings are for.'

'Sorry,' Melanie apologised, 'I should have——'

'Thought?' he supplied, and scooping up the binoculars and sextant, turned towards the hatch. 'Come on.'

Her heart gave a great leap. She was going to dive! But at the bottom of the steps Luke handed her the instruments. 'I'm going to get kitted up. Take these to my cabin.' He fished the notebook out of his back pocket and thrust that into her hands as well. 'Make sure they can't fall off. Then come back to the diving room.'

Her dashed hopes rose again. 'You mean I can go down with you?'

'No,' he said bluntly, 'you're not diving today.' She was surprised by the depth of her disappointment. 'I want you to pack a marker buoy and two lines with five- and ten-metre marks for decompression stops. The echo Callum had is at twenty metres and we probably won't be down long enough to need them, but there's no point in taking chances.'

'What about a compass and depth gauge?' Melanie was brisk, fighting down her disappointment. After all, this was only a location dive to mark the wreck, if it was the wreck.

'I'll wear both on my wrists. Put the rest of the stuff in a nylon mesh bag. I'll want a large torch as well. Is Derek ready?'

'Yes.' As she passed the diving room she heard Derek ask Luke if she would be diving. She hurried on, knowing the answer but not wanting to hear it again. How could he be so casual? she wondered as she put both binoculars and sextant into their cases and laid the notebook on the chart beside the station pointer. He might have been diving for seashells instead of being the first person to see a ship that had lain on the ocean floor for two hundred and fifty years.

As she got back, Luke emerged from behind the rack clad in the bottom half of a scarlet wetsuit. 'While we're down, Melanie, I'd like you to start keeping a detailed log.' He slung the jacket on to the bench and strapped a knife to his thigh. The sight of his naked brown torso, his wide shoulders and deep chest, the dark curly hair spreading down over his flat stomach, gave Melanie a peculiar jolt. She turned away quickly, searching the shelves for the torch he wanted. Paul had never tanned; his skin was always pale, but after they had pulled him from the water it had been a greyish colour, tinged with blue, and that was how she remembered it. When the nightmares hurled her back to the night before he died and she relived the sensation of his arms round her, they were cold and clammy, like the tentacles of an octopus. She knew her mind was playing tricks, that in her dream the latter event had become superimposed on the earlier one. For in reality he had been hot and slippery with sweat, and she hadn't been able to break his hold. She had fought, but he had crushed the breath out of her and then——

'Melanie?'

She started. Luke was staring at her. His eyes were slightly hooded and she flinched inwardly, curling away from their laser-sharpness like a sea-anemone from a probing finger. 'Did you hear what I said about the log?' His tone was curiously gentle.

Her mouth was dry and her lips stuck to her teeth as she spoke automatically. 'Yes, of course.' She moved quickly along the shelves to pick up a nylon bag, aware of his thoughtful gaze following her.

'How's the tide?' Derek peered through the viewfinder on his camera.

'High, and we're just into slack water now.' Luke zipped up his jacket, buckled on his weight belt and lifted the cylinder harness on to his shoulders. 'We won't have as long as at low tide, but the visibility should be better.'

'I'm sweating like a pig,' Derek complained. 'Do we really need to wear all this stuff? Last time I dived in the Indian Ocean it was lovely and warm.'

Luke grinned briefly. 'It's not for warmth, it's for protection. We're diving on the fore-reef and we don't know what the currents are like down there. If you get brushed against the coral you can lose a layer of skin before you even realise it. There's also the wreck itself. If it's there it will be encrusted with razor-sharp marine growth.' His smile grew wintry. 'I would prefer not to have blood in the water so early in the proceedings.'

Melanie shot him a puzzled glance, while Derek looked sheepish. 'Sorry, I should have realised.'

'Realised what?' she asked.

'Sharks,' was Luke's succinct reply. 'Can we go now?' He picked up the bag and his fins and left the room.

Without stopping to think, Melanie ran after him. 'What about repellent or something?' she demanded breathlessly.

He turned and faced her. 'What about it?'

'Well, shouldn't you take some?'

'If we don't bother them, they won't bother us, and I've found that a clout on the nose discourages far more effectively than chemicals.'

Melanie blinked as the full implication of his statement sank in. 'Oh, terrific.' She folded her arms. 'For you to bash a shark on the nose it has to pretty close—too close for comfort or safety. *Your* hands might be free, but Derek will have his full with the camera. Anyway, aren't you the one who was so concerned about insurance? What are you trying to do? Get your money's worth from having a doctor on board?' She had spoken recklessly, but she didn't care. Derek would be a sitting target for any inquisitive or hungry predator. Her mind refused to recognise the real direction of her concern.

'Don't be ridiculous,' he snapped. 'In my opinion, and I'm the one with experience, there'll be no danger from sharks on this dive. Now get that log organised and stop behaving like—like a woman!'

Melanie's chin came up and her eyes sparked. 'Why? I *am* a woman,' she retorted immediately.

Luke's glowering expression softened momentarily. 'You certainly are,' he said softly, and started up the ladder to the stern deck, leaving her staring after him.

Callum had edged the boat forward and dropped anchor. The engines were silent and the boat rode the long swell easily. The only sounds Melanie could hear as she emerged on deck were the cries of the seabirds, the sighing of the wind and the rushing hiss of the waves breaking over the reef twenty yards away.

Luke and Derek had their masks in place and as Melanie checked her watch and marked the time on the sheet clipped to the board she held, Derek stepped over the gunwale and on to the broad ladder leading down to the water. He paused to pull on his fins and put the demand valve in his mouth. Luke handed him the camera and Derek slid into the water and finned slowly to the stern where a marked and weighted rope would guide them to the bottom.

Luke checked his own watch and picked up the bag, then looked at Melanie. 'We'll be up in thirty minutes,' he said, then followed Derek over the side, entering the water with barely a splash.

'Good luck!' she called. He gave a brief wave and dived.

The next half hour seemed interminable to Melanie. She thought of going below, of checking the medical supplies and facilities in the tiny sick-bay. She debated going to the day cabin and looking at charts of the area, knowing, as she sought activity, that a king's ransom would not tempt her from the deck.

As the boat lifted and fell, she stared down into the luminescent blue-green depths. Shoals of tiny silver fish darted to and fro. Other fish, larger and of varying shapes, meandered about, their brilliant colours dimmed by the light-filtering effect of the water. Once she thought she glimpsed a shadowy figure, but she couldn't be sure. Her eyes ached from trying to pierce the sun's glare on the water beyond the stern. She realised that Callum would not have anchored directly over the wreck partly for safety, in case the anchor dragged, and partly because the boat's shadow would have limited visibility for the divers.

How she wished she were down there with them! She loved the freedom of movement, the effortlessness. And in these waters especially, there was so much to see. She would go down tomorrow, on that she was determined.

'Hey, Mel, you asleep?' How long do I have to hang about here?' shouted Derek from the stern line.

Melanie ran to the ladder and leaned over to take the camera. 'Is it there? Did you find it?' Even in her excitement, force of habit reminded her to check her watch and record the time on her sheet.

'Looks like it.' Derek hung on to the ladder, removed his fins and slung them on to the deck.

'Where's Luke?' Melanie peered down at the water.

'Right behind me. He's just attaching the buoy.' As Derek spoke, a bright orange sphere tossed to the surface a few yards beyond the rope, and several moments later Luke's head appeared.

As he clambered back on board, the demand valve bumping against his chest, he dropped his fins and peeled off his mask. Melanie held her curiosity and excitement tightly under control.

'Well?' demanded Luke. 'Nothing to say? We found her. Our first run and we hit her spot on! Callum'll get a bottle of rum for this.' A broad smile lit his face. It was the first time he had allowed himself to reveal how much it meant to him.

'But of course,' Melanie shrugged, wide-eyed, resorting to irony in an effort to mask the startling impact of Luke's smile. 'With your deductions from the records and Callum's technical expertise, how could you miss? After all,' one corner of her mouth tilted impishly, 'she wouldn't have dared move.'

Slowly, deliberately, Luke swung round. Though his expression revealed nothing, his eyes flashed a warning which was part threat, part promise. Her nerve ends tingled and she swallowed reflexively.

Derek smothered a grin and picked up his camera. 'I'm off to get this film processed. I'll have a sandwich in my cabin. Mel, be a love and rinse my gear for me.' He flashed a winning smile and without waiting for a reply stepped through the hatch. 'See you both at dinner.' The words floated up behind him.

Luke took his cylinder harness off and laid it gently on the deck. 'Before you do that, go and tell Callum we're right on target and to make the co-ordinates.' He unzipped his jacket and pushed the hood back. His black hair was wildly rumpled and his skin looked even darker against the scarlet. 'After you've rinsed the suits and cylinders, come down to the day cabin.'

'Yes, *sir*,' Melanie replied tartly. He turned a slow gaze on her but said nothing. He hooked his thumb into the waistband of his skin-tight wetsuit trousers and pushed them down towards his hips.

With as much dignity as she could muster Melanie turned and started towards the bridge. She was furious. She should have stood her ground. Why had she fled? She was a doctor, for heaven's sake; she had seen naked men before. But he wasn't just any man, he was Luke Avery. A man who stirred terrible memories, and provoked violent conflicting emotions.

She was still smarting when she returned to the day cabin. Dressed once more in shirt and jeans, his hair roughly combed and curling thickly on his neck, Luke was bent over the table marking fixes on a chart.

He glanced round as she entered, but his attention was centred on the wreck as he straightened up. He tapped his chin with the pencil then turned to face her, tossing the pencil on to the chart. Leaning back against the table, he folded his arms. 'It would have to have been a particularly low tide when she struck,' he said thoughtfully. 'Her keel seems to be wedged in a crack in the coral. She must have been smashed down by a heavy sea. She'd have been overwhelmed in seconds.' He reached over the table and picked up a large leather-bound volume. It looked very old, the leather cracked and faded in places. Luke opened it. 'According to this, the ship *Buckingham* escaped the Marati by running before a storm.' He frowned. 'Why didn't she stand off and make for deep water? In rough weather she'd have been far safer doing that than staying close to shore.'

'Perhaps she was trying to reach Fort Dauphin?' Melanie suggested. 'Maybe her master or some of the crew had been wounded?' Her irritation was forgotten as she visualised the three-masted ship pounded by driving rain and a boiling sea, her canvas shredded by howling winds as her terrified crew seized their only hope of deliverance from the most brutal pirates in the Indian Ocean by sailing into the teeth of a storm. She shivered. What a terrible choice! They had lost their gamble and paid with their lives. 'I only hope it was quick,' she muttered.

'What?'

She shook her head. 'Nothing. Was there something

you wanted me to do?'

He nodded, turning to look at her. 'Will you work out the maximum time we can stay down doing two dives a day, both at slack water? The currents and tidal flow are too strong at any other time.'

'Have you some paper and a pen?'

He gestured. 'Help yourself. On the desk. You'll find tide and decompression tables there too. Remember, I want to avoid decompression stops if at all possible.'

'That will limit your bottom time.' Melanie glanced up from making notes to find he was still watching her, his level gaze intent, his dark brows drawn together in the suggestion of a frown.

'I know,' said Luke, 'we'll have to plan the dives carefully, and get in and out as quickly as we can.'

'Did you check the depth when you were down?' She felt her cheeks grow warm. Why was he looking at her like that?

'Twenty metres at the lowest point. She's on a slope. It's high water and we're in the spring tides at the moment, so this is the deepest it will get.'

Melanie's pen flew over the page as she worked on the calculations, but part of her mind was occupied not with figures, but by the quizzical expression she had seen in his eyes.

'I shall go down again about five this afternoon to fix the guide lines and work out an approach for tomorrow.'

She looked up. 'Is Derek going down with you?' Luke shook his head. 'But you should never dive alone into a wreck, that's a basic rule.' The words were out before she could stop them.

'I'm not going into the wreck, I'm only fixing guide lines,' he said patiently.

Melanie shrugged. She wouldn't ask again, not today. To be turned down twice would be too much. 'You're the boss.' She looked down at the figures and so did not see his mouth twitch. 'Tomorrow morning high tide will be at eleven-thirty. You have about half an hour's slack water either side of that time, and forty-five minutes on the bottom.'

'Fine, thanks.' Luke turned back to the chart table. 'What will you want me to do?'

He lifted one shoulder. 'Make sure the log is kept right up to date. You could also help Callum with the cylinders.'

'No.' Melanie smiled. He had misunderstood. 'I meant what will you want me to do when we dive?'

Luke straightened slowly. 'You're not diving.'

'Not today, I know,' she began, 'but——'

'Nor tomorrow,' he interrupted quietly.

Melanie's head snapped round, then dropping the pen she swung to face him, disappointment vivid in her widening eyes. Her throat felt tight and she swallowed hard. 'What do you mean? Why not?' Barely eighteen inches apart, they stared at one another. His face was stony, an implacable rock against which the tide of her hurt and bewilderment broke and fell away, leaving no impression.

'Because I say so. And as you so rightly put it, I'm the boss.' Luke's voice was perfectly calm.

Her anger surged through her. 'That's not fair!' she cried. 'You have to give me a reason. I'm a fully qualified diver. I'm damned if I'm going to be used as a dogsbody! I know to begin with you expected a man. If you remember, I was prepared to leave. *You* hired me, *you* persuaded me to stay. Why did you bother if you won't let me do the job you're paying me for?' Her breath came unevenly and her heart was pounding with the force of her fury and frustration.

Luke's jaw had tightened during her outburst.

'On your last working dive there was an accident. A man died.' He raised a hand to forestall her. 'You were cleared of all blame—I'm not questioning that.'

Melanie was bewildered. 'Then what's all this about? I've had a medical and I've done test dives. I'm perfectly fit.'

'Physically, I'm sure you are.'

She swallowed. 'And what's that supposed to mean?'

'Whatever else you may think, my first priority on this mission is the safety of the people on this boat. That includes you.'

'But I——'

Luke put both hands on her shoulders. 'You wouldn't knowingly imperil anyone, I know that,' he said gently, searching her face. 'But we're in a potentially dangerous situation, and I can't take chances. You're going to have to tell me what happened.'

Melanie's thoughts raced. Her face felt stiff. Luke's fingers were burning through her thin shirt. She tried to edge away, but he held her fast and his grip did not falter. She stared at his chest. 'Paul—we were doing a test dive at forty metres. We'd been down fifteen minutes when he started showing signs——'

'Of nitrogen narcosis,' Luke said impatiently. 'I know all that, Derek told me. That's not what I meant.' He tightened his grip, and instantly her hands came up to ward him off. 'Before that, Melanie. The day before, the night before, something else happened. What was it?'

Her lips were paper-dry and she felt the colour drain from her face. He couldn't know, he *couldn't*. It was just a guess. 'I—I don't know what you're talking about,' she whispered.

He shook her, not hard, but his exasperation was evident. 'Don't lie to me, Melanie. I told you before, I'm neither blind nor a fool. While you're bottling up this whatever-it-is, the stress could affect both your judgment and your reflexes. Retrieving the cargo from that wreck is going to be physically demanding and extremely hazardous. We're also running against time. With pressures like these I can't compromise safety, so unless you tell me the truth, you stay out of the water. It's up to you.'

CHAPTER FIVE

MELANIE'S body remained absolutely still, but her thoughts ran wildly in all directions, desperately seeking an escape. She couldn't tell him, it was impossible. But to be tied to the boat for several weeks and not dive? That was impossible too.

The hardest thing to face was the knowledge that he was right: the stress *was* beginning to tell. But only in the last two days, only since he had come into her life. Before meeting Luke Avery she had coped. Now she didn't know what to believe. It was he who had stirred the mud, brought all the memories so horribly alive. Yet he had done it without, until now, asking a single question. He accepted her as a scientist, yet made her all too aware of herself as a woman.

For an instant she was tempted. Emotionally exhausted by outrage and a crippling burden of guilt, she no longer knew which was real. In this morass of confusion she had nothing to cling to, no one to tell her if she was right or wrong. But who could help? There was only her word.

What if she told Luke everything, the whole dreadful story? No, she simply couldn't. Even now, she could imagine behind the conventional expressions of sympathy a glimmer of doubt, a hint of accusation.

As if he sensed the battle raging within her, his grip tightened. Her shoulders ached beneath the pressure of his fingers. 'Melanie, I'm trying to help.' His voice was rough. 'Trust me.'

She wanted to, so much. She was tired and he seemed kind. She looked up. His features were blurred by her tears. She swallowed the hard lump in her throat. 'The night—the night before Paul died, I was working late in the lab writing up results of experiments we'd done that day. Everyone else had gone, including Paul. We'd had another disagreement earlier. It wasn't anything serious——'

'Another disagreement?' Luke interrupted. 'Did they happen often?'

Melanie chewed her lip. 'No—yes—well, they had got more frequent lately. They were mostly about work.' She hesitated.

'Mostly?' prompted Luke.

A tear spilled over and trickled down her cheek, and she quickly lowered her head and wiped it away. 'There . . . there were other things, personal . . . anyway, I was just getting ready to leave when Paul came back. He'd obviously been brooding on what he seemed to think were my deliberate attempts to sabotage his work. You see, Paul was a go-getter, full of confidence, ready to try anything.' Her voice wobbled. Luke slipped an arm around her shoulders, passed her his handkerchief and drew her to his side as he leaned against the desk. Melanie wiped her nose and crushed the cotton square into a ball. 'He was clever, but he had no patience. He wanted quick results and in his opinion the experiments we were doing were taking too long. He wanted to push ahead, cut corners, take risks. But for that particular series I was in charge. There's no denying he had obtained some terrifically useful data. The programme had taken a big step forward, but there'd been some hair-raising moments, and it scared me. I'd had it drummed into me all through my training that the safety of the divers was top priority, that you didn't take risks that jeopardised yourself or your partners. So I couldn't go along with his methods.'

'But that wasn't the only thing on his mind.' Luke

made the words a statement, not a question.

'No,' whispered Melanie, twisting the handkerchief round and round. 'We, that is Paul and I, had been seeing quite a bit of each other socially.' She broke off, not knowing how to continue.

'Was it a serious relationship?' Luke asked quietly.

'We weren't engaged or anything like that,' Melanie's voice cracked, 'I was fond of Paul, but I knew he wasn't the right person for me on a permanent basis, and he had no intention of getting tied down, as he put it. But he—he wanted more from the relationship than I was willing to give. It led to problems.' Tears blinded her once more as she struggled on. 'That night, he'd been drinking and he got wilder and wilder. He—we had a terrible row.' Even now she could remember feeling too sick and shaken afterwards to drive her car. She had phoned for a taxi and huddled in a corner of the back seat, ice-cold and trembling. His parting shot, as she had lain bruised, stunned with helpless rage and humiliation, had been a threat to have her branded indecisive and over-cautious and replaced as dive master for the rest of the programme.

'When I saw him next morning, he seemed quite normal, though we didn't talk.' It had taken every ounce of will-power she possessed to re-enter the laboratory. Her stomach had contracted and for one dreadful moment she had thought she would vomit. But she had clung to the doorpost, sucking in air, and the feeling had passed. He had entered a few minutes later, already wearing his wetsuit, avoiding her eyes, brisk and breezy with the technicians as they handled the cylinders and helped him get kitted up.

'It was an important test in the series and we were using the deep tank. When everything was ready I went to get changed. When I got back about ten minutes later, and I was told that Paul had already gone down, I thought he was just determined to make his point, to do it his way. Then Lars, one of the technicians, said Paul had told him to give me a message.' Melanie was fighting for control.

'What was the message?' Luke prompted.

She closed her eyes tightly. 'Just one word: Sorry. Right after that someone shouted that Paul was behaving oddly and his responses weren't making sense. I signalled him to abort the dive, but he wouldn't come up. So I went down, but I couldn't—it was too late.' Her head was down and her chest heaved with the sobs she was choking back.

'Was that all that happened, Melanie? The row and his drinking?'

She stared at him. Should she? Oh God, she couldn't. 'Isn't that enough?' she cried. 'He's dead!'

Cupping her chin, Luke gently forced it up. 'And you think it was deliberate.'

Melanie flinched. She had carried the secret fear for months, but to hear it voiced in a bald statement shook her. Pressing her lips tightly together, she nodded.

'You're wrong, Melanie. That row had nothing to do with Paul's death—at least, not the row itself, and certainly not directly.'

'How can you be sure?' she whispered.

'Look. He broke the rules once too often. You never drink the night before a dive. It was the alcohol in his system that triggered the nitrogen narcosis. His judgment was impaired before the dive, and the effect of compression at depth exaggerated that. Biochemistry, Melanie. His death was an accident, a genuine accident.'

'But the message——'

'A grudging apology. The Paul you described would never have killed himself over a quarrel, no matter how serious, believe me. The man was too much of an egotist. And even he must have realised he couldn't get you fired for obeying safety regulations. He was probably trying to backtrack. Don't give it any special significance, Melanie. It deserves none.'

With all her heart she wanted to believe him. Even allowing for what she hadn't been able to say, it still made sense. Paul alone had been responsible for the tragedy, but it had not been a deliberate act of self-destruction. He had simply taken one risk too many.

Luke's hands were gentle as he drew her round to face him, but his voice was unexpectedly harsh. 'Let it go, Melanie. Leave it in the past where it belongs. It's over, finished.' With his thumb he wiped away an errant tear that trembled on her lashes. She looked into his eyes and beyond the compassion in their blue depths she saw something stir. He whispered her name. His gaze held hers and her heart turned over as his head came down. His lips brushed her temple, her cheek, and rested momentarily on the corner of her mouth. They were warm, the kiss tender, and she felt a rush of longing. But as her eyes closed, the fear surfaced. Her hands clenched, all her muscles went rigid and icy sweat dewed her body.

Luke moved back, a puzzled frown drawing his dark brows together. There was a knock on the door, and in the same instant the intercom buzzed.

She sprang away from him and walked quickly towards her cabin. 'Melanie, wait,' he said tersely, then called 'Come in,' as he pressed the intercom button. 'Avery.' She hesitated by the inner door. Please, no more questions, she prayed silently.

Callum's voice crackled. 'Can ye come forrard, Luke, Billo says there's a message for ye on the radio.'

'On my way.' He turned to the steward. 'Yes, Herbie?'

'Will you lunch here, sir, or in the saloon?'

Luke held Melanie's gaze. She could see the questions in his narrowed eyes and a determination to obtain answers. 'In the saloon. Dr Driscoll is coming now, I'll be

along in a few minutes.' One corner of his mouth lifted in
the ghost of a smile. 'Ask François to make sure Dr
Driscoll eats well. She's diving tomorrow afternoon.'

'Yes, sir.' Herbie nodded and closed the door.

Luke's mouth twisted. 'Why so surprised? Trust works
both ways.'

'Thanks.' It was totally inadequate, but she couldn't
think of anything else to say.

'I'm going to see Callum. I'll catch up with you later.'

'Luke,' she said quietly as he opened the door, 'I won't
let you down.'

He turned from the doorway and looked at her over his
shoulder. No smile hovered about his lips now, his face
looked almost stern. Then she met his eyes and the
tenderness in them startled her.

'I know,' he said with quiet conviction, and went out,
closing the door softly behind him.

She stared at it for several seconds, aware of a slow,
subtle upheaval taking place within her.

He still hadn't arrived by the time she had finished her
meal. François had fussed over her like a mother hen.
She managed two helpings of rice and prawns, but when
he brought in extra fruit, she rebelled. 'I'll burst, or I'll
sink like a stone, and it will be all your fault!'

François merely tutted, screwing his eye up against the
ever-present curl of smoke. Privately Melanie had to
admit she felt physically better and more at peace with
herself than she had for days. The crushing burden of
guilt had gone.

With Luke busy and Derek yelling at her not to open
the door as the prints would be ruined, she spent the next
hour finding a wetsuit that would fit her, rigging up a
harness for herself with twin-cylinders, and fitting hoses
and a demand valve. Then she went down to the
compressor room. Callum arrived a few moments later
and gave her a sceptical look when she told him she could

manage alone if he had other things to do. But after he had watched her check the oil levels, drains and valves, then change the filter, he shrugged, muttered 'Aye, well', and with a brief nod left her to it.

She had just finished charging the cylinders and was entering the shut-down time in the log when the intercom buzzed. It was Callum. 'Ye're wanted in sick-bay, lassie, young Alain's burned hissel' on the oven door.'

The burn wasn't very large, but blisters had already formed and Alain looked pale. François hovered, his affection for his nephew obvious despite his continual carping. 'All zis fuss, ice-cubes and bowls of water, cream and dressings. When I am young, we just rub on butter.'

'And cook the burn,' Melanie said mildly. 'Cold water takes out the heat and pain and reduces the risk of infection and scarring. That's more than butter ever did.' She pinned the bandage. 'I'll look at it again tomorrow, Alain, just to see how those blisters are. How does it feel now?'

'All right, sank you,' the boy replied in heavily accented English. He flexed his hand carefully.

'Good. Now I want you to have a warm drink and something to eat.'

'Eh? What is zis?' François glared suspiciously at her. ''E is not on 'oliday. 'E 'ave work to do.'

'Of course he does,' Melanie agreed. 'But you don't want him dropping things because he feels ill, do you? Even small burns can cause shock. Now, if Alain does as I tell him, in half an hour he'll be ready to get on with his chores. OK?'

'OK.' François removed the smouldering butt from his mouth and eyed it with irritation. He jerked his head towards the door. 'Allez, mon brave, ze doctor, she 'ave spoke.' But as he stumped out ahead of his nephew, Melanie read suspicion and protest in every line of his short figure. Alain glanced back uncertainly, and Melanie winked and waved him away. He flashed her a grateful grin and followed the muttering François back to the galley.

Dinner that night was an eye-opener for Melanie. Callum and Billo joined them. It was the first time Melanie had met the engineer's mate, who doubled as radio operator. A Scot, like Callum, and about the same age, he was a reserved, softly spoken man whose thickset body seemed at odds with his fine-boned, rather studious face. Introduced by Luke, Billo shook her hand. But his greeting, though polite, was formal rather than warm. Were all the Scots such a misanthropic lot, Melanie mused as Herbie served her with succulent lobster, or was it just the natural reserve of any close-knit group towards a newcomer?

With Derek on one side, Luke on the other and Callum and Billo opposite, Melanie was surprised to see Herbie and François seat themselves at the table. They were served by Alain, who then joined them on the end. The conversation was lively and full of jibes. Even Derek took his share of goodnatured teasing. Only Luke and herself were exempt. Luke, she guessed because in spite of his easygoing manner and approachability, he was still the boss. And herself? She supposed it was partly because she was the only woman present, and partly because she didn't belong—yet.

When the debris of the meal had been cleared and Alain had poured the coffee, Luke signalled to Derek, who reached under his chair and brought out a large envelope. The banter died away as all eyes fastened on it.

'Here she is,' he said, and tipping the photographs out, handed them round. Encrusted with weed, sponges, barnacles and shellfish, it was hardly recognisable from some angles as a ship. The masts and bowsprit had gone. Much of the deck structure had been smashed, probably when the masts fell. But the shape was unmistakable.

Luke leaned towards her, and she quivered inside at the warm pressure of his thigh against hers. 'I've attached guide lines here and here,' he pointed. 'There's a certain amount of silt on the wreck. But keeping fin movement to a minimum will help.' Acutely aware of him, Melanie nodded, gazing fixedly at the photographs.

'How're ye going tae get in?' asked Callum, studying the prints one after another.

'I'm not sure yet,' Luke replied. He laid several photographs on the table. 'Part of the hatch here has been broken away and appears to have jammed inside.' Everyone craned forward to see. 'There's a gash in the hull I might use, but I'll have to check the measurements, I don't know if I could get through with cylinders. Anybody got any suggestions?'

Melanie listened as ideas were tossed back and forth. Alain asked a question about lights which was answered by Derek, and Billo's query regarding the layout of the wrecked ship had them all huddling even closer as Luke pointed out the various compartments and the likely whereabouts of the cargo they sought.

Later Melanie closed her cabin door and leaned thoughtfully against it. The reason for the crew's loyalty to Luke was obvious. Every single one of them had been at dinner; they all knew what had been found and what was planned. She herself felt she had a personal stake in recovering the cargo. Though only Luke, Derek and herself were actually diving, the others were just as important, their roles just as vital to the smooth running of the operation, and Luke had conveyed that without saying a word. Melanie smiled in admiration as she prepared for bed. As he said, he was no fool.

She was woken the next morning by a brisk knock on the door and Luke's voice calling, 'Move yourself, breakfast in ten minutes.' She looked at her watch; it was almost seven. She stretched, sighed happily and bounded out of bed. Today she was diving. She'd see the wreck for herself.

While they ate, Luke gave her a list of things he wanted done, she added her own suggestions with which he agreed, and they went their separate ways. But every so often she found her thoughts straying from her work, recalling things he had said and the play of expressions across his strong features.

As the day wore on Melanie felt excitement begin to grow in her. The sun began its descent towards the mountains and the shadows grew longer. Huge billows of grey cloud piled up and the rain fell in torrents, drumming on the deck and streaming down the Plexiglass portholes.

At a quarter to five she went to the diving room. She had purposely gone a little early hoping to change in private. She had just pulled on her wetsuit, which was black with an orange stripe from armpit to ankle, when Derek breezed in. 'Hi, sis, ready to go?'

Melanie zipped up her jacket. 'You don't know how much I've looked forward to this.'

Derek started to strip off. 'I think I can guess,' he grinned.

Luke walked in. He looked her over. 'Is that suit comfortable?'

She looked down at herself, then nodded, 'Fine, thanks.'

He walked towards the rack and as he passed her, remarked, 'It fits well.' She glanced at him in surprise. One dark brow lifted enigmatically, then he deliberately allowed his eyes to roam over the swell of her breasts, down to her narrow waist and long slender legs all clearly defined by the suit that clung like a second skin. She grew warm under his appreciative gaze, half of her shy, wanting to turn away, the other half proud and slightly bemused by her own femininity. He caught her eye and she glimpsed a wicked gleam as he lifted his own suit out and hooked it over the rail. He loosened his shirt from the waistband of his jeans and in one lithe movement, pulled it over his head. Melanie's heart thumped and she turned away. While she buckled on her weight belt and hauled her cylinder set on to the bench, Derek checked the waterproof casing on his camera. She was strapping a knife to her calf, her hair falling forward like a gold curtain, when Derek called her name. She looked up and blinked at the flash.

'Just testing,' he smiled, lowering the camera. She pulled a face at him. Then Luke, zipping up his jacket, said casually, 'Keep that print for me.'

Derek raised both eyebrows at Melanie, who shrugged helplessly and leaned over the bench to pick up her harness.

'Here,' Luke was suddenly beside her, tall, powerful and much too close. 'Let me help.' He took it from her.

'I can manage, thanks,' she said quickly.

'Of course,' came the dry rejoinder, 'but on my boat we follow the rules. I check your harness and buckles, you check mine.'

'Doesn't anyone care about me?' Derek cried plaintively.

Melanie giggled. 'Fool! I'll check you in a minute.' Luke made her operate the quick-release on her weight belt, and she made a point of taking just as long checking his gear. It was quite easy working at the back, examining the valves on his cylinders even though she had to ask him to bend his knees so she could see properly. But when he turned so she could check the buckles and release mechanisms she was burningly conscious of his steely eyes watching her every move. She could see the rise and fall of his chest, feel his warm breath on her cheek, slow and even, and it took enormous will-power to control the tremor in her fingers. But despite the effect he was having on her, she was determined he would have no chance to criticise her professionally. She finished and stepped back, glowing pink under his unblinking scrutiny, but aware from the ironic twist to his mouth that her point had been made. Laughter bubbled inside her. 'That's it,' she said blithely, avoiding Luke's eye, and turned to her brother while Luke collected the rest of his equipment.

'He fancies you.' Derek's whisper held a mixture of surprise and amusement.

'Don't be ridiculous!' hissed Melanie, her face aflame. 'He's just observing regulations.'

'Is having a photo of you in the regulations too?' Derek's mock innocence was more than Melanie could take. She stood on his toe.

'Ouch!' he yelped.

'When you're quite ready.' Luke's brisk tones brought them both round. 'We'd better be prepared for poor visibility once we start moving about on the wreck. Derek, you attach a line to the stern rope, you'll need more freedom than us. Melanie, you'll be on a buddy-line with me.' He picked up his fins, torch and the bag containing safety lines and tools. 'Let's go.'

When Melanie emerged on deck the downpour had stopped. The air smelled sweet and fresh. The mountains brooded beneath a pearl and primrose sky. Wraiths of pink and orange cloud reflected the dying sun. She stared, entranced.

'Spectacular, isn't it?' Luke said over her shoulder. 'However, there'll be another one tomorrow, and we're on limited time.'

They completed their preparations, checking the signals they would use underwater, and with Derek leading, Luke second and Melanie bringing up the rear, entered the water. They trod water while Derek looped

one end of his line round the stern rope, the other round
his wrist, and snapped the clip shut. Then taking the
camera from Luke he switched on the lamp strapped
around his helmet and disappeared beneath the swell.

Melanie slipped her gloved hand into the loop Luke
held out, and watched as he put the other end over his
own wrist. She felt an odd sensation in the pit of her
stomach. For the duration of the dive they would remain
joined by a rope six and a half feet long. Automatically,
Melanie checked her watch. They had just over an hour.
Luke was watching her. She adjusted her mask, took a
slow, steady breath from the demand valve and raised
her hand, the thumb and index finger forming an O,
signifying all was well.

The sun had gone. Dusk had crept in from the east,
bringing with it a full moon which washed the dark,
rolling water with silver. Luke returned the signal and, as
one, they dived.

He did not switch his torch on, and she wondered why.
Then as they finned slowly down, she saw sparks and
flashes emanating from him as though he were surrounded by electricity. It startled her, and she was about
to tug on the line when she realised that he knew, and was
giving her a chance to see the phosphorescence given off
by the plankton as their passage through the water
disturbed the minute animal and vegetable organisms on
which the coral fed. How thoughtful he was!

A few seconds later Luke switched on his torch. She
did the same, and suddenly, against the grey-black
backdrop of the ocean, the reef stood out, vibrant with
colour. There were plate-like corals of sapphire, green
and yellow, pink lace fans and crimson-twigged
branches. Among them nestled purple sponges caressed
by ribbons of golden weed. Blushing sea-anemones
waved fringes of tentacles gently on the current. Fish
surrounded them. Ordinary fish-shaped fish, coloured

emerald, turquoise and lemon, with ruby stripes and inky
dots. There were fish that looked like lumps of coral, and
spiky ones like sea-urchins. Some fish had long fins that
rippled like frilly chiffon, and others had tails like
pincers. Some bounced slowly along like small, bright
balloons, others darted, pencil-like streaks of silver.

Melanie was entranced, then she felt a gentle tug on
the line. A few feet away Derek hung in the water, hardly
moving. Ahead of them lay the wreck, clearly visible in
the torch beams. She forgot everything else as they
moved closer. The ship lay tilted slightly on one side,
resting on a gently sloping bed of coral which fell away to
uncharted depths beyond the stern.

She saw the guide lines Luke had fixed at regular
intervals along the deck, so no matter how murky the
water got, they would not lose contact with the wreck.

Drifting slowly over the ship behind Luke, Melanie
looked for possible ways in. They made one complete
circuit, then Luke pointed to the hatch and mimed lifting
out the broken timbers. She nodded and they placed their
torches either side of the jagged hole and started work.

It was difficult and tiring, and the rope joining their
wrists made things even more awkward. Once, in sheer
desperation, she reached for the loop, intending to pull
her wrist free, but Luke's hand clamped over hers. He
shook his head violently. After a little while they
developed a rhythm which had them working in unison
instead of pulling in opposite directions. As the water
grew cloudier, Melanie clipped a safety rope from her
other wrist to one of the deck lines. She took the
splintered planks Luke passed to her and laid them
gently on the canting deck. Silver bubbles streamed in
regular bursts towards the surface as, despite the physical
efforts demanded, both kept their breathing steady and
even. She glanced up and caught his eye. He winked and

she felt a great burst of happiness, but she stifled it at once.

She was amazed when she checked her watch to see their time was almost up. She tugged on the line and when Luke emerged from the almost clear hatch, pointed first to her watch and then upwards. She could see he was reluctant to leave, but discipline won.

Luke motioned Derek down to get what pictures he could, then Melanie unclipped the safety line and they headed slowly towards the surface.

The single deck light showed Callum waiting to help them back into the boat. As Melanie clambered over the gunwale, she spat out the demand valve and ripped off her mask, unable to contain her excitement. 'Callum, it's fantastic down there, and we're almost ready to go in!'

She unbuckled her harness and he took the twin cylinders off her back, shaking his head. 'I dinna ken what Luke's thinking of,' he tutted.

Melanie flashed him a delighted smile. 'I know, you "dinna hold wi' lassies aboard", but you'd be surprised Callum, I'm quite useful to have around.'

'Aye, well,' the engineer grudged as he laid the cylinders on the deck, 'mebbe.' He glowered at her, then one eyelid fluttered in what might have been a wink, and he turned to help Derek.

Showered and changed, Melanie carried her suit up to the deck to rinse it. She was just coiling the hose when Derek came throught the hatch.

'Don't put it away, I've got to do mine and Luke's.'

'Getting in well with the boss?' she teased.

Derek made a rude noise. 'As a matter of fact he usually does his own, but he's just got another of those ever-so-private radio messages.'

Melanie looked up. 'What do you mean?'

He shrugged. 'They come through in code. He doesn't send Billo out, but he does insist on taking them himself.'

As she fitted her suit on to its hanger, Melanie's forehead wrinkled in curiosity. 'What do you suppose they're about?'

'Who knows?' Derek played the hose over the two suits. 'Mafia? Secret agents? Or perhaps it's just some gorgeous female wanting to know why he's stuck out here instead of sipping champagne in her boudoir.'

Melanie laughed, but the effort it cost surprised her.

Dinner followed the same pattern as the previous evening, though the talk was more general as there was little new to report regarding the wreck. Melanie waited but Luke didn't mention the radio messages and no one asked. She couldn't help wondering. If everything else was common knowledge, why not that? Unless of course they were too personal to share. She shied away from the thought and concentrated on the conversation.

'We should at least get inside tomorrow,' Luke was saying, and at once Melanie felt her imagination caught. It would be like going back in time. They would see how the men on that ship had lived, the instruments they had used to navigate, and ordinary things like cutlery, furniture and even materials, if they hadn't been totally destroyed by the water.

She smothered a yawn. It had been a long, busy day, the best since her arrival, and tomorrow promised even more. Excusing herself quietly, she slipped away to her cabin.

Nodding over her book, a thriller she had selected from the bedside shelves, she heard Luke enter the day cabin and move about as he prepared for bed. She closed the book, switched off the light and snuggled down. Her last waking thought as she settled herself more comfortably, was of the rope joining her wrist to Luke's as they worked to clear the hatch.

Two hours later the nightmare began. It started as it always did with Paul's face, mottled with fury, hurtling towards her like an express train through a tunnel. But instead of jerking her awake, it trapped her, terrified, unable to move as the now-familiar, gut-wrenching pattern unfolded. The row, the struggle, her screams, his ragged groans, churning water and great bursts of air bubbles boiling upwards. Then Paul's eyes, blank, his cold, blue-white flesh and his gaping mouth coming closer and closer.

Her own scream woke her and she shot upright, drenched with sweat, as Luke, still tugging on blue cotton pyjama bottoms, burst through the door and scooped her into his arms.

Uncomprehending, still caught in the web of her nightmare, Melanie fought like one possessed, gasping and sobbing. But he held her to him, seeming impervious to the blows she was raining on his arms and shoulders.

'It's me, it's Luke, you're safe,' he repeated over and over again, cradling her head with one hand, his other arm crushing her against his bare chest.

Consciousness returned and her terror gradually subsided, leaving her shaking uncontrollably.

'It's over,' he murmured against her temple. 'You were dreaming. You're quite safe.'

She tried to stop shaking, but her body wouldn't respond. Awareness of his arms around her, his body heat as he held her close, his skin against hers above the thin straps of her nightgown, had the fear welling up again. She struggled for control. 'I'm all right,' she panted, shrinking away.

But his arms were iron bands. 'Not yet,' he said softly, 'but you will be, soon.' He stroked her hair slowly and gradually a little of the tension left her.

'I'm sorry,' she mumbled, her face buried in the warm hollow of his neck.

'For waking me? Forget it, you were having a bad time. It wasn't me you were dreaming about, was it?'

'No,' she shuddered. 'Why?'

'You were calling my name.' The unexpected comfort of his closeness and the rhythmic sweep of his hand down her head and neck was so soothing that for a moment Melanie didn't grasp what he had said. When it sank in she stiffened, and pulled her head back to look at him. Her cabin was in darkness. The light from his spilled through the doorway, illuminating part of his face, making his eyes gleam like a cat's.

'No,' she swallowed, 'you must be mistaken. I couldn't have.'

'I'm not mistaken.' There was no doubt in his quiet reply. 'The question is why do you jump like a scalded cat whenever I touch you, yet call my name in your sleep?' He laid her back on the pillow, then placing his hands either side of her head, leaned down.

The bedclothes were tumbled about her hips, and Melanie clenched the sheet in her fists as she stared up at him, eyes wide, hardly breathing. She was rigid with apprehension, yet tormented by a treacherous longing to be in his arms once more, to be safe. *Safe*? How could she even think that? What was safe about Luke Avery? Hadn't he threatened her peace of mind since the moment they met? She must be losing her reason.

Luke's mouth brushed hers, once, twice, as light as a breath. Then he drew back, his eyes glinting as his gaze swept over her slender figure, lingering on her breasts, half-exposed by the damp, crumpled cotton nightgown.

He stood up. 'Get some sleep, Melanie.' His voice was husky. 'I'll see you in the morning.' The door closed behind him.

In the warm darkness Melanie stared at the ceiling, grateful that he had left her, yet oddly bereft. She closed her eyes, reliving the sensation of her cheek against Luke's chest, the silky-roughness of the hair, the pounding of his heartbeat in her ear, the warm strength of his arms and his musky fragrance. As she realised what she was doing she blocked the thought out and turned over, searching for a cool place on the pillow. But again and again the memory returned and she touched her mouth with tentative fingers. His kiss had been so light she had scarcely felt it. She wished—*no, she mustn't. It was too dangerous*. She turned over again, but it was a long time before she slept.

CHAPTER SIX

MELANIE was wakened by a tap on the door. Before she could ask who was there it opened and Herbie walked in carrying a tray. He set it down on the foot of the bed, and as he drew back the curtains, she sat up, hugging the sheet against her. 'What time is it, Herbie?' She rubbed her eyes.

'Six-fifteen, miss. The Captain says he and your brother are diving in three-quarters of an hour if you feel up to joining them.'

Picking up the cup of steaming coffee, she smiled at the steward. 'Thanks. Please tell him I'll be in the diving room in thirty minutes.' She left the chilled fruit, but spread the croissants with guava jelly and chewed slowly. If she felt up to joining them. Was that veiled criticism or sympathy? Whose idea had the breakfast-tray been? She recalled the aftermath of her nightmare. Luke had said she called his name. Try as she might, she couldn't remember doing it. But he wouldn't have lied, would he? What would be the point? It had been the same dream that had haunted her for four long months. Nothing in it had changed. So why had she called out the name of a man she had known only a few days? What tricks was her subconscious playing?

She was still, her coffee cup poised half-way to her mouth. Did she somehow hope Luke Avery could change things? That was impossible. Nothing could alter what had happened. Yet something *had* changed. She no longer felt guilty, and that had been Luke's doing. He had divined the terrible suspicion she had been unable to voice, and had shown it to be completely unfounded. She would always be grateful to him for that.

Gratitude? a little voice inside her mocked. Was it
gratitude that had kept her awake long after he had
returned to his cabin? Gratitude that caused her to relive
again and again the sensation of his arms around her, the
roughness of his chest, the musky freshness of his skin?
Was it gratitude that edged aside her paralysing fear on
finding herself clasped against a man's body? Or was it
the stirring of something else—something she couldn't
identify because she had never experienced it, had
believed that after that terrible night she never would?

She crashed the cup down on the saucer and stumbled
out of bed. Her knuckles were white as she turned on the
taps and raised her eyes to the mirror above the small
basin. Stop it, she told herself. Stop it. *Stop it!*

There were shadows in the soft brown eyes that stared
back at her, but the pallor had gone, and the honey-toned
skin no longer stretched quite so tightly over the high
cheekbones. 'What's happening to me?' she whispered.
The reflection had no answer.

Luke and Derek were already in their wetsuits when
Melanie entered the diving room.

It was impossible to avoid Luke's eye and her colour
heightened beneath his hooded scrutiny as she recalled
not only the aftermath of her nightmare, but her own
deliberate clinging to the sensation of being in his arms.
Swallowing the painful dryness in her throat, she
managed a croaky 'Good morning,' her lashes fluttering
down to veil her eyes.

Luke's answering 'Good morning,' sounded calm,
almost indolent, but having caught his eye once, Melanie
wasn't fooled for an instant.

'Hi, Mel.' Her brother gave a huge yawn and shook his
head. 'God, my skull is stuffed with cottonwool this
morning!'

'You're not coming down with a cold, are you?' she

asked in concern, unutterably relieved at having something to steer her thoughts away from Luke Avery.

He inhaled deeply. 'My nose is clear and my throat is
fine.' He grinned at her. 'What do you bet we'll get a
change in the weather?'

The rainy season's not due for weeks,' Luke countered,
'and according to Billo, this morning's forecast is good
clear sky, light breeze, good visibility, just the conditions
we need.' His eyes swung back to Melanie, unspoken
questions clear in his vivid gaze. She looked away
quickly, willing him to say nothing, especially in front of
her brother.

Derek tapped the side of his nose. 'We'll see. I'm just
going to fetch my other camera. I'd like to get some cine
film as we go into the wreck before you both start moving
stuff and turn the water into soup.' He went out.

Melanie went behind the rack to change.

'What does Derek know about weather changes?'
called Luke from the shelves.

'It's an old family joke.' Melanie sprinkled herself
liberally with talcum powder and the close-fitting
trousers slid easily up her legs and over her hips. 'During
school holidays when we were young my parents would
fix up picnics or trips to the beach. I loved the water even
then and Derek has had his own camera since he was
seven. But every so often, just as we were about to get in
the car, he'd look up at a clear blue sky and announce
that it would rain before lunch.'

'And did it?'

'Every time.' Melanie zipped up her jacket and pulling
her hair loose from the collar, walked to the bench where
Luke had laid out her harness. 'It was quite uncanny.'

'Much as I respect your brother's talent as a
photographer, so far as his weather predictions are
concerned, I'll take my chances with the meteorological
satellite.' Luke caught her hand and pulled her round

gently to face him. 'Are you all right?'

She looked up at him. One dark brow slanted sardonically, mocking their conversation, leaving her in no doubt that he had recognised her desire to avoid any reference to the previous night. Yet there was no mistaking the concern that deepened the lines on his forehead and either side of his mouth. 'Of course, why? Shouldn't I be?'

'You were very upset last night.'

She looked away from his probing gaze, keenly aware of the strength in his fingers as they curled around hers.

'It was just a bad dream,' she whispered. 'Everyone has them.'

Luke's expression was grim. 'Not like that they don't.' He hesitated. 'Melanie, you don't have to prove anything to me. There's no rule that says you have to dive every day.'

'But I want to,' she said earnestly, 'and I'm all right, I promise.'

'OK. Got everything?' She nodded. 'Then let's go.'

Derek went in first, moving slowly, filming continuously as Luke and Melanie waited outside the wreck. Luke pointed to the huge gash in the planking and she understood the warning. She could feel the suck and blow of the current as water was drawn in and out of the hull. While they waited for Derek, Melanie went down to examine the keel. Shining her torch along the bottom of the ship, she saw that where it rested on the coral, the wood was smashed. Luke had said the ship was wedged in the reef and indeed it did appear so, but Melanie wondered. Many of the oak timbers had become as hard as iron during their two and a half centuries trapped on the fore-reef, but much of the other wood had crumbled away to dust.

Luke tugged on the line and Melanie finned gently upwards in time to see Derek emerge from the hatch. He waved Luke on, but, pointing at his sister, shook his head. Luke reached for his end of the buddy-line and she shot forward, clamping her small hand over his wrist and the rope, shaking her head angrily. He wasn't going to leave her behind. She was as much a part of it as they were. Through the masks she held his gaze, telling him with her eyes she wanted to go with him, that he *had* to let her. She willed him to understand and, after a long moment, he nodded. Releasing his wrist, she followed him down into the darkness of the wreck.

They were entering amidships, and as soon as he had reached the bottom of the stairs, Luke turned towards the stern where the Captain's quarters would be, attaching a safety rope as they went. They passed an open doorway. Melanie shone her torch in and recoiled as two grinning skulls leered at her from a tangle of bones and shreds of cloth. With an effort she kept her breathing steady. She should have expected that. If the ship had been overwhelmed so quickly by the storm, few of the crew would have had any chance of escape.

They reached the door of the Captain's quarters. It was closed. Luke tried the handle, but it wouldn't budge. Melanie squeezed alongside him and added her weight, but they could not shift it. Their efforts had stirred up the silt and the water had become thick and cloudy. Luke signalled a return to the surface and, frustrated by this unexpected barrier, they retraced their route to the hatch.

As they emerged into clear water, Melanie caught a movement from the corner of her eye—one moment there, the next gone, leaving only the memory of a dark, slender shadow.

'How many more bodies do you think we'll find?' asked Derek as they discarded their equipment in the diving room. Behind the rack, quickly pulling on her shirt and jeans, Melanie listened for Luke's answer.

'It's hard to say. The sharks will have had most of them. But we won't know about the Captain's cabin until we can get that door open.'

'It can't be locked, surely?' Derek was rubbing himself down with a towel. 'I mean, who would barricade themselves inside a ship which was about to sink? Mel, you're the doctor, have you ever heard of such a thing?'

Flicking back her wet hair, she picked up her suit and walked across to collect the rest of her equipment for rinsing. 'I'm no psychiatrist, but I know in threatening situations people sometimes do behave irrationally.'

'You see weird things in the papers,' Derek mused. 'People dashing out of burning houses clutching a child's toy or a favourite saucepan.'

Luke added his suit and harness to the growing pile in the centre of the floor. 'That's not so irrational.' He tossed his fins on top. 'It's not the things themselves that are important, it's the security they represent—that's what the people are really clinging to. I'll do the rinsing. Melanie, get the log up to date and make a record of all the photos we've got so far. Use my desk. I'll see you both at lunch.'

Melanie worked steadily through the rest of the morning.

Herbie poked his head round the door to announce lunch. Thanking him, she went into her own cabin to wash her hands and comb her hair. What was this cargo they were looking for? Surely he'd have to tell them soon. It was odd that no one had asked. Or maybe it wasn't. Maybe they had already been told. Maybe she was the only one still in the dark. She'd settle that as soon as a suitable opportunity presented itself. But a suitable opportunity meant being alone with Luke Avery, and did she really want that? She paused, the comb forgotten. She felt torn. Questions crowded her mind. Was he really descended from Lucas Avery, the nineteenth-century pirate? If so, what was his motive for retrieving the cargo? Money? The upkeep of the boat and wages for the crew must cost him plenty, yet though his clothes and personal possessions were of excellent quality, he appeared to regard them as purely functional. He certainly didn't give the impression of being short of money. The boat was extremely well equipped and the crew devoted to him, all signs of a healthy financial state. In fact money didn't seem to enter into it at all. Then why was he doing it? Was it some sort of vendetta? Was he determined to finally capture what his ancestor had lost? And why shouldn't the *Buckingham* have been carrying it? Who had pulled the strings to short-circuit the rules governing salvage? Did the coded messages have anything to do with it?

She laid the comb down. Who *was* Luke Avery? Each day she became more aware of him. She had only to be in his presence and all her senses were heightened. She must fight it. But how?

Luke, Derek and Billo were already eating when Melanie arrived just ahead of Callum. When Luke stood up and beckoned her to her usual place between Derek and himself she hesitated, but only for an instant—after all, a communal meal offered no threat. She sat down and with a slightly unsteady hand ladled some fish stew on to her plate, knowing in her heart of hearts that she was losing the will to fight.

'I hate to say I told you so,' said Derek.

'And I can't stand people who gloat,' Luke cut in. Though his tone was mild it had enough of an edge to bring a slight flush to the younger man's face. 'This could be serious.'

Melanie looked up quickly. 'What is it? What's happened?'

'It hasn't yet,' Luke said, 'but unless we're damned

lucky——' He broke off.

Alarm stirred in her as she looked around the table. 'Will somebody please tell me what we're talking about?'

'There's a deepening depression to the east of us,' Billo's quiet voice relayed the devastating news in the level tones of a professional broadcaster. 'Which, with other conditions, is forming a cyclonic storm centre.'

'Isn't that the kind where winds move in a gigantic circle?' Derek asked, and Billo nodded.

Melanie's mind raced as she realised what this could mean to the mission. 'Could it miss us?'

Billo and Callum exchanged glances. 'Aye, it's possible,' Billo said. 'If it veers north, we may just catch the edge.'

'What sort of winds would we get then?' she pressed.

Billo thought for a moment. 'Mebbe force six or seven.'

'That's approaching forty miles an hour,' Derek frowned.

'I've no fears for the boat,' said Luke. 'We've ridden far worse than that. But we're very close to the reef, and a combination of low tide and deep troughs could be risky.'

Melanie recalled that it was in exactly those conditions the *Buckingham* had sunk. She thought of the grinning skulls and shuddered. 'How long before this storm reaches us?'

Billo scratched his head. 'It's no' easy to say. Four hours, six?' He shrugged. 'With these ye canna tell.'

Luke pushed his half-full plate away. 'Derek, don't eat any more—you can't dive on a full stomach and we're going down in an hour.'

'I'm coming too,' Melanie said at once.

'No,' Luke said abruptly. 'Derek won't be filming. We have to get that door open and we'll be using cutting equipment, so there'll be no room for you.' She flushed painfully at his brusque rejection. Callum and Billo looked down at their plates and Derek's eyebrows rose in surprise.

Melanie swallowed. Pride kept her head up and her voice steady. 'If you stay down the full length of your no-stop time, you might need extra air. I'll go and rig a couple of spare breathing sets, just in case. Will you need cylinders for the cutting equipment?'

As he rose and towered over her she saw a strange, warm light in his eyes and her heart gave a peculiar flutter.

He shook his head. 'I've got a portable pack all ready for use.'

On deck the two men finished their preparations. Melanie shaded her eyes as she looked at the restless water. The hot sun tipped it with gold and a gentle breeze lifted her hair. Yet there was a tension in the air like the crackle of electricity. Was it just her imagination? She stared out to sea, screwing her eyes up in concentration. Instead of the usual clear line at the horizon, a narrow strip of dark blue separated sea from sky. It puzzled her, then she realised it was a wall of cloud. She opened her mouth to warn Luke, then closed it again. He would already have seen it and taken it into account. Instead, she noted it in the log, with the time. She would remain on deck and keep an eye on the speed of its advance.

Derek gave her the 'thumbs-up' and went down the ladder. Luke passed down the cutting equipment and followed him into the water. As they disappeared beneath the rolling swell, a gust of wind, like a giant's laugh, pressed into her back, and despite the heat, she shivered.

The minutes dragged by. Melanie watched the wall of cloud draw nearer. The breeze had stiffened and was now quite fresh, the gusts more frequent. She looked at her watch. They had been down almost half an hour. As she turned her back to the wind to note the time on the sheet, she caught sight of the two spare cylinder sets she had brought on deck. Even if Luke and Derek did stay down to the limit of their time, it was only another fifteen minutes, so they should have plenty of air to spare. She wasn't sure why she had bothered with the extra sets. Maybe she was over-cautious. But they weren't doing any harm just sitting there. She looked out towards the south-east once more. The leading edge of the approaching front was no longer a clean, dark line; swathes and streamers of cloud ran before it, an indication of the speed and force of the winds driving it landwards from its mid-ocean spawning ground. The air had lost its crystal clarity and the sea was an opaque grey-green.

She looked at her watch again, then heard Luke's voice calling her name. She spun round, a smile lighting her face as she saw him by the stern line. 'Thank goodness! It's started to look really nasty up here.' She reached down to take the cutter. 'Did you get the door open? Where's Derek?'

Luke had taken his mouthpiece out, but hadn't removed his mask. 'Derek's trapped,' he said without preamble. 'I need a spare breathing set.'

Melanie went cold. 'Is he hurt?'

Luke shook his head. 'Not badly, just a gash on his leg. Hurry with the cylinders.'

Snatches of disjointed thought tumbled through her mind as she heaved the cutter over on to the deck and ran across to collect one of the harnesses. Derek would be shocked and using up his air supply all too quickly as his breathing rate went up. Blood in the water would attract sharks, and the storm was getting closer every minute.

'How long will it take to get him out?' She handed the set down.

'Can't say. It's not dangerous, just awkward, and I'm working as fast as I dare.'

'Luke, what about your air? And tools?'

'I'm OK.' A wave slapped against his face. He spat and shook his head. 'Tell Callum to get the engines on standby. We must get off this reef as soon as I get Derek out.'

'I'll come down,' Melanie said quickly. 'I can help——'

Luke didn't let her finish. 'You bloody well stay where you are!' he roared. 'I've got enough to worry about. You stay put, that's an order, Melanie.' He clamped the mouthpiece between his teeth and vanished.

'Luke, listen——' But he had gone. As she straightened up the wind whipped her hair across her face, making her eyes water. The gusts were growing stronger and the waves were tipped with foam.

'Oh God,' she whispered, and flew along the deck to the bridge. Callum was perched on a swivel chair behind the wheel, watching the hunched figure of Billo fingering various dials on the radio, but all he could pick up was the hiss and crackle of static.

Both men swung round as she crashed through the door, and the look on her face brought Callum to his feet. 'Derek's trapped in the wreck,' she gasped. 'Luke says you're to get the engines on standby ready to move the boat off the reef as soon as they surface. Billo, what's the latest on the storm?'

He shook his head in disgust. 'I canna get a thing, too much interference.'

Icy fingers clutched at Melanie's heart, followed by a surge of anger so fierce it almost choked her. To hell with Luke's commands! How dared he give her orders to stay safely on board whilst her brother was *trapped*? She was trained to deal with situations like this. She'd handled emergencies before. Adrenalin flooded her bloodstream, charging her with energy and resolution.

'Callum, I'm going down. If Luke can't get Derek out in ten minutes he'll be cutting the safety margin of air in his own tanks too fine. Rig me a safety line so I can signal you, and get some shark repellent—Derek's injured. I'll also need gauze wadding and a wide bandage from sick-bay to try and contain the bleeding. And see if you can find a large polythene bag and a wide elastic band.'

Now the decision was made, her anxiety for her brother, her fury with Luke, and the unidentifiable emotion that threatened to suffocate her when she thought of the risks he was running, were relegated to the back of her mind.

Callum and Billo exchanged glances, but all Callum said was, 'Aye, lass.'

'Meet me in the diving room, I'm going to get kitted up.' She opened the door to the deck and the wind tore it from her grasp, slamming it back against the superstruc-ture. She grabbed it and hauled it almost shut, shouting above the wind's howl. 'Billo, will you go and keep an eye on the stern line in case they make it before I'm ready to dive.'

He followed her along the deck which heaved as the boat pitched and rolled on the waves.

Melanie had never changed so fast in her life, yet it felt as if she were moving in slow motion. Automatically she checked her equipment and tested the valve, her breathing regular, her fingers steady.

Callum arrived with the pads, bandage and polythene bag rolled and fastened with the elastic band. He handed the package to her without a word and she stuffed it together with a saw, a long crowbar and spare rope into her mesh bag. She slipped a knife into the sheath strapped to her calf, and picked up her fins.

When they reached the deck, Callum clipped the safety rope around her waist, while she adjusted her mask after tucking her hair into the close-fitting hood. She looked hopefully at Billo, praying all the prepara-tions were for nothing, as he lifted his eyes briefly from the stern line. But he shook his head.

After Callum had sprayed her all over with shark repellent and dropped several more of the small canisters into her bag, she clambered over the side and on to the ladder. The waves were much higher now. One moment there were four rungs visible below the one Melanie was standing on, the next water reached her thighs as she fitted her fins and placed the demand valve in her mouth.

'Good luck, lassie!' Callum shouted gruffly as he took the second breathing set from Billo and looped it over her arm, followed by the bag and lastly a torch.

She took a quick look at her watch, put her hand over her mask to hold it in place, and as the next wave surged along the side of the boat she stepped off the ladder.

Once below the surface the visibility was better as she followed the guide rope down. But the murky cloud surrounding the stern half of the ship told its own story. Melanie sensed she was being watched, and she peered around her. At the limit of her vision, torpedo-shaped shadows slowly circled. She counted three, moving lazily, propelled by the occasional flick of a tail, the grey bodies streamlined and sinuous, revealing the flash of a white belly as they passed and re-passed one another. Each circuit brought them fractionally closer.

Letting go of the guide rope, she grabbed one of the repellent canisters. Pointing it at the sharks, she ripped off the metal tab and the chemical was discharged into the water in a burst of compressed air. She could only hope it would mask the scent of Derek's blood and keep them away from the wreck long enough for her and Luke to get him out. She knew with an awful certainty that she would need the other canisters and could only hope there were enough.

She switched on her torch and went into the wreck. It was incredibly difficult to avoid hitting things with the spare cylinders plus the bag clutched in one arm and her

torch in the other. She had to move slowly, constantly
aware of the weight of her own cylinders, wary of
snagging her suit or hoses on the sharp edges of broken
timbers or splintered bulkheads.

Eventually she reached the Captain's stateroom. The
door was closed, but she could see a neat square where
the iron lock had been cut out. She pushed hard and it
swung open. She could see the two men beside a tangle of
planking. Broken chairs, a large upended table and two
tall chests were piled haphazardly on one another. Part of
the ceiling had collapsed and the cabin was in chaos.

She signalled Callum that she had reached them and so
far all was well, and after receiving the acknowledgment,
moved very carefully towards Luke.

He grasped her shoulders, his expression thunderous.
She was deeply shaken. Surely he could see she had no
choice? She held out the fresh breathing set, pointing to
her watch. He released the almost empty cylinders and
she helped him on with the new ones. As soon as the
straps were over his shoulders he waved her away,
pointing towards the surface, but she shook her head
vigorously and moved over to crouch beside her brother,
who was trapped face down a couple of feet from the
floor. When she touched his shoulder he twisted round
and gave her a 'thumbs-up', which irrationally brought a
lump to her throat. She shook her fist at him, then shone
her torch along his body and down to where his leg
disappeared in the broken planks. The water was too
cloudy for her to see how much blood he was losing. She
had a fleeting vision of the lazily circling shadows outside
and knew the repellent would not keep them at bay for
long.

Luke had obviously removed some of the timber, but
not enough to free Derek, who couldn't lever himself out
without the strong possibility of the taller of the two
chests falling forward and crushing him.

Catching hold of Melanie's arm, Luke mimed what he intended to do and what he wanted from her. She nodded quickly.

First he wedged the door open—Melanie assumed they had closed it to keep out any inquisitive shark while they searched the cabin. He left the bag beside it, then while Melanie positioned herself at Derek's head, clasping him under the arms, Luke pushed the crowbar under the plank imprisoning Derek's leg. As he pressed, the plank lifted, but as it did so, the chest tilted forward a fraction. Melanie caught her breath, then forced herself to exhale. Nitrogen was building up in all of them. Steady even breathing was vital if they were to avoid narcosis. She *had* to keep her nerve, remain calm and follow Luke's instructions. Her brother's life depended on it.

Once more Luke pressed carefully down on the crowbar, and the plank lifted a little more. Melanie eased Derek forward. She felt him flinch and knew he was in pain. Luke increased the pressure and she pulled again. They moved in fractions of an inch. She kept her eyes on the chest. It had not moved again, but that only made her more nervous. As each second passed and she edged Derek closer to freedom, she expected it to come crashing down.

They were almost there. A quick, anxious glance showed Melanie that the physical strain of raising the heavy plank millimetres at a time was beginning to tell on Luke. Suddenly Derek shook his head and pointed urgently down his leg. Instantly she realised what the problem was. He was still wearing the broad rubber fin and couldn't turn his foot to free it.

Not pausing to consider the risk, Melanie released him, and laying her body alongside his she reached down towards his feet. The heavy chest leaned drunkenly over her as she manoeuvred her hand into the gap alongside his ankle, wrenched off the fin and let it fall. Then back in her original position she quickly grabbed him under the arms once more, nodded to Luke who made one final effort, and tugged Derek free and, dragging him with her, finned desperately towards the doorway.

As soon as she waved the torch to let him know they were safe, Luke released the crowbar, and using every ounce of power in his legs, kicked after them. As he reached the doorway and Melanie reached out to haul him through, the chest tumbled forward slowly and crashed to the floor, splintering to matchwood the planks that had held Derek captive. The shockwave hit them like a blow and they clung to one another as the dust of centuries rose in the water in a thick dark cloud.

Luke retrieved Melanie's torch from Derek and held it while she quickly bound the dressing around the four-inch gash in her brother's leg, before pulling the polythene bag over his foot. She squeezed as much water out of it as she could, securing it below his knee with the rubber band.

As soon as she had finished she signalled Callum they were on their way up and pressing one repellent canister into Derek's hand, she passed one to Luke, keeping two for herself.

With Derek between them they made their way through the ship to the hatch. Motioning them to wait, Luke went out first. A couple of seconds later he beckoned briskly and took Derek's arm to help him upwards.

Melanie checked her watch. Luke and Derek had run fifteen minutes over their permitted no-stop time. According to the safety regulations they should wait for thirty minutes at a depth of five metres for the nitrogen to be released from their bodies.

Scanning the water around her, Melanie saw the dark shapes closing in. They were restless and there were more of them, and she knew no stops would be possible; Luke and Derek would arrive at the surface with tiny bubbles of nitrogen fizzing in their blood like deadly champagne.

She was so concerned about them she didn't notice one smaller shape detach itself from the rest and rocket upwards, until the sleek body hurtled past, almost touching her. She recoiled violently and almost screamed. With trembling fingers she tore the metal cap from the repellent and as the shark arrowed in a second time, she held the canister at arm's length, directing the stream of chemical straight at it. The shark suddenly veered off, and almost sobbing with relief, she kicked upwards.

They broke surface into a maelstrom of wind, spray and heaving water. Rain lanced down in sheets from low, fast-moving clouds. Billo hauled on her safety line and Luke lifted her bodily on to the ladder. Her legs were like jelly as she landed on the deck next to Derek. She shrugged out of her harness, ripped off her mask and leaned down to help her brother. He was deathly white but attempted a grin.

'Let's go to the Antarctic next time,' he stuttered through chattering teeth, 'it's safer, only polar bears and icebergs!'

She tried to keep the urgency out of her voice. 'Let's get that leg fixed. You and Luke have to start decompressing in twenty minutes at the outside.'

She helped her brother to his feet and glancing over her shoulder saw Luke speaking to Billo as they collected the gear together, following her down as she assisted a limping Derek to the sick-bay.

He was shaking badly and she had to help him strip off his wetsuit. Billo arrived with warm clothes and helped him dress except for trousers while Melanie swabbed his leg with antiseptic then injected a local anaesthetic. Billo took the suit away and Melanie inserted eight stitches in the jagged wound.

'I'll see that François has hot soup and sandwiches ready as soon as you come out of decompression,' she told her brother, noting that he kept rubbing one shoulder, wincing as he flexed it.

Melanie bandaged the wound as fast as she could. Pains in the joints after too long at depth were a sure sign of the dreaded 'bends'. Just as she was finishing, Luke, now in jeans and a warm sweater, walked in, filling the tiny room with his presence. He did not look at Melanie, but leaned over and hoisted Derek to his feet.

'Start hopping, sunshine, we've just run out of time.'

Melanie followed them down to the recompression chamber. She could feel the engines vibrating through her feet and the changed motion of the boat told her they were heading into the waves away from the treacherous shallows of the reef.

Billo was waiting and helped Derek into the chamber, which resembled a giant cylinder lying on its side in a cradle. While sprawled on comfortable seats inside, he and Luke would be subjected to the same pressure they had experienced at wreck depth. In just under an hour this would gradually be reduced until all the nitrogen had been released and their blood chemistry was completely normal.

Now the crisis was over and she had done all she could, Melanie suddenly felt desperately tired. She shivered as she watched Luke climb into the chamber. He had not spoken a single word to her since they'd come back on board. She longed for some sign of recognition of what they had achieved, just a word, a glance. Between them they had saved Derek's life, *surely*——

He twisted round and her tentative smile froze. His eyes were glacial. 'Billo can handle this. Get some warm clothes on and a hot meal. I'll deal with you later.'

CHAPTER SEVEN

SHE could not have been more shocked if he had slapped her face. Billo busied himself with the valves, carefully not looking at her. Melanie's eyes filled; she turned quickly and walked out.

By the time she reached her cabin she was shaking, partly from reaction now that the crisis was over, but mostly from an almost unbearable hurt.

Stripping off her wetsuit, she wrapped herself in a thick terrycloth robe. She hadn't been looking for praise; she had simply done what was necessary. They had all been in grave danger and she had been terrified. All she had wanted from Luke was a smile, or a wisecrack, to release the tension and minimise their brush with death. She picked up her sponge bag and went into the shower. As the hot water flowed over her head and body she gradually relaxed. A deep sigh shuddered through her and tears trickled unnoticed down her wet face.

But as she towelled dry, recalling for the tenth time Luke's icy, arrogant tone and bleak expression, something in her changed, and the hurt was drowned in a growing anger. So he'd deal with her later? *Like hell he would!* Who did he think he was, God? So she had disobeyed an order. She'd had no choice, and she would do exactly the same again.

Tying the robe firmly about her, she returned to her cabin. As she reached the outer door, Herbie appeared with a laden tray.

'Compliments of François, miss.'

Melanie opened the door for him and followed him through the day cabin and into her own. She slung her sponge bag on to the bed and lifted off the metal cover. The fish in its spicy sauce steamed on a bed of fluffy rice. There was also a jug of fresh fruit juice and a glass. 'Thank you,' she said absently, still preoccupied with her thoughts.

Herbie set the tray down on the foot of the bed. Melanie sat down, and picking up the plate and a fork, began slowly to eat.

'And may I add my own sincere congratulations, miss.'

Melanie glanced up, puzzled. 'For what?' she asked between mouthfuls.

Herbie removed the sponge bag from the bed-cover and placed it carefully on the edge of the basin. 'What you did, miss, diving like that—with the storm an' all, it was very brave.'

She stared at him, her fork poised halfway to her mouth. 'Herbie, that was my brother down there!'

'Even so, miss, it took a lot of nerve.'

Melanie shrugged awkwardly. 'I didn't really have time to think.' She turned her attention to the plate, feeling the hot food restoring her.

'That's not what Callum says.'

She looked at the steward. 'Oh?' she said carefully. Had she upset the dour Scot? In her anxiety she had issued orders left and right. Had Callum, who was obviously Luke's second in command, and who had never approved of her being on board, taken offence?

'He said that for a lassie you're a good man to have around.'

Melanie's eyes widened. 'Callum said that?'

Herbie's grin was tinged with apology. 'That's our engineer, all charm.'

Her face lit up. 'You know what, Herbie? That's the nicest compliment I've ever received.'

'I'm sure it won't be the last, miss. No doubt the Captain will have something to say when he gets out of that machine.'

Melanie's smile faded, but she said nothing.

'Can I bring you anything else, miss?'

'I'd love a cup of coffee.' She put the empty plate back on the tray. 'Please thank François—that was absolutely delicious, and I certainly was ready for it.'

'I'll tell him, and with your permission, miss, I'll see to these.' He bundled up the clothes she had discarded earlier, folded the wetsuit over his arm and, picking up the tray, went to the door. Melanie opened it for him and with an impeccable bow, Herbie left the cabin.

She dressed quickly in a clean shirt and fresh jeans. Her hair was almost dry and she combed it into its usual side parting. It fell soft and shining to her shoulders, the fringe feathering across her forehead.

The warm glow that suffused her was not due entirely to the delicious meal she had just eaten, or to the hot shower. Callum had accepted her. Not only that, he had been open about his change of heart.

'So to hell with you, Luke Avery,' she muttered, and went out into the day cabin. But as she sat down at his big untidy desk, she felt a pang of misery. Her defiance was an empty shell. Surviving a situation such as the one they had faced created a unique bond between people. Yet he had chosen to ignore it. What a fool she had been, imagining he considered her an equal, imagining—she closed her eyes tightly, then pulled in the chair.

Picking up a pen, she began entering details of the dive in the log. Herbie brought her coffee, and a plate with two dainty fruit tarts on it. 'Alain made them himself, miss, he wanted you to know.'

Melanie tasted one. She was pleasantly surprised; the pastry was featherlight and the fruit tangy. 'It's lovely.' She wiped a crumb from the corner of her mouth. 'Please thank Alain for me, and tell him I'll see him in sick-bay,' she glanced at her watch, 'at five, to change the dressing.'

Herbie grinned and left.

Melanie ate the second tart and drank her coffee. The crew on this boat had raised diplomacy to an art form. Had Alain's little gift been his own personal compliment to her, or simply a reminder that she had promised to see him again today? As it happened, it had slipped her mind, but she would certainly remember now.

Pushing the cup and saucer aside, she went back to her writing. She was partly through the incident with the shark on their ascent, when the door opened and Luke strode in, slamming it behind him.

The abruptness of his entrance made her jump. His features were taut and his eyes glittered like chips of ice. Melanie swallowed the sudden dryness in her throat and her fingers tightened on the pen. Her heart thudded against her ribs, but she did not speak. If there was to be a row, then he, not she, would have to start it.

But he didn't say anything, he simply stared at her. Then from deep in his throat came a sound like a groan, and reaching out he seized her shoulders and hauled her bodily out of the chair. Melanie gasped, but the sound was cut off as his lips crushed hers. His arms went round her. One hand gripped the back of her neck, the other slid down her spine, moulding her against him.

Too stunned to react, Melanie arched, pliant and supple against his hard-muscled body. He tore his mouth away. 'You could have been killed!' he rasped against her ear.

Her knees turned to water and to stop herself falling, she clutched at him. She had expected anger, recriminations, restatement of his authority, but nothing had prepared her for this. 'So—so could you,' she stammered, forgetting to dissemble, revealing the anxiety that had tormented her as much as her brother's predicament.

He held her closer, pressing his lips to her temple, her cheek, her hair. 'That was my responsibility.'

Aware of what she had said, and of Luke's acute perception, she tried to prevaricate. 'He's my brother.'

'And my employee.'

'But your air——

'I had enough.'

'You didn't have any shark repellent.'

'True.'

'Or a crowbar, or—or a polythene bag.'

'I know, I know. But I would have got him out, Melanie. It would have taken a few minutes longer, but we'd have made it.'

'So you didn't need me at all.' Her attempt at lightness had a hollow ring. 'And my efforts were quite unnec——'

'What you did,' he cut in hoarsely, 'was very brave. But if you ever take such a risk again, I'll——' He broke off.

She raised her head to look at him. The force of his feelings emphasised the planes and angles of his face. His expression was harsh, threatening. 'You'll what?' she asked quietly.

He stared into her eyes for a long moment. 'I don't know.' He shook his head slowly. 'I've got no imagination, have I? You're a qualified diver, used to exercising authority, and you can handle a crisis.' He cupped her face gently between his hands. 'But you frightened the hell out of me.' This time his kiss was tender, cherishing, and in the kaleidoscope of her confused emotions a key turned, and her heart opened like the fragile petals of a spring flower. Her mouth softened and grew warm. Her fingers uncurled and spread against his shirt. She could feel his heart pounding and his skin hot beneath the thin cotton. It wasn't the disobeyed order that mattered, it was *her*. He cared about her. She hardly dared believe it, wary of accepting what, in a blinding flash of clarity, she knew she yearned for.

The old fear hovered, black and malevolent, on the fringes of her mind, but her blossoming joy kept it at bay.

She was infused with a new inner strength and peace. Now, instead of simply accepting his kiss, she returned it, at first tentatively. But when, feeling her response, he groaned softly and his mouth grew more demanding, her arms crept upward and locked around his neck.

'Luke,' Derek's voice accompanied a brisk tapping on the door, 'you got a minute?'

Luke raised his head. 'Can't it wait?' His voice was husky and impatient.

But Melanie shook her head and freed herself from his arms, though her eyes never left his. They were both trembling, their breathing fast and ragged. She laid her fingers fleetingly on his lips in a gesture that expressed the intoxicating mixture of trepidation and delight that had exploded within her, and for which she had no words. But she needed time, time to adjust, to comprehend. He seemed to understand for, seizing her hand before she could withdraw it, he kissed the tips of her fingers, then indicated the inner door.

'Luke?' Derek called again.

Safely inside the cabin, Melanie leaned back against the door. Still breathless, she felt light-headed, but bursting with a happiness almost impossible to contain.

She heard Luke open the door, and the low rumble of voices. Then the intercom buzzed, there was more conversation, and a moment later Luke knocked on her door. Moving quickly away, she called 'Yes?'

He opened it. 'Your brother would like a word, it seems his leg's giving him trouble.' The warmth in his eyes made her heart kick. His expression was bland, but a self-mocking quirk at one corner of his mouth told her that pretence went against his nature. He was humouring her, she knew, allowing her to set the pace, and she thanked him with her smile.

He stood back to let her pass. 'I'll be on the bridge most of the night. We'll return to Fort Dauphin at first light.

With a sea like this running, diving will be out of the question for at least thirty-six hours, so we may as well take the opportunity to have a break.'

'Oooh, land—something firm to stand on, and a bit of room to move!' Derek grinned, rubbing his hands together, but his gaze was speculative as it shifted from Melanie to Luke and back again.

'I'll see you in the morning,' Luke said casually to Melanie.

She nodded. 'I must go and see to Alain's arm.'

'What about my leg?' demanded Derek. 'Aren't you going to——'

'Of course I am,' she broke in soothingly, and linking her arm through her brother's led him out of the cabin. 'And I'm quite sure you will tell me exactly where, why and how it hurts and what you expect me to do about it.'

'Some bedside manner you've got!' he accused. 'You have no idea what I went through.'

'Oh, I think I have,' she retorted lightly, 'I was there, remember?'

'Only part of the time,' he corrected.

'The important part.' Luke's deep voice floated over their shoulders as he followed them down the passage. 'She got you out.'

'Look, let's not get sidetracked by insignificant details,' Derek complained, 'I'm injured and in pain. I don't think I'll be able to eat any dinner.'

They stopped outside the sick-bay. Luke passed them and strode on down the passage, and Melanie forced herself not to watch him go. She opened the door and went in, and going straight to the basin washed her hands, then started setting a tray with dressings, scissors, antiseptic and bowls. 'Come off it, brother, I've known you too long, it will take more than a few stitches to put you off your food. Besides,' she tried not to smile, but the corners of her mouth kept lifting, 'Callum, Billo,

François and Alain are going to be pretty annoyed if you don't give them a firsthand account of what happened down there. Luke won't have the time if he's going to be on the bridge sharing the watch with Callum all night.'

Derek's face brightened. 'Yes, I suppose I owe it to them really. I mean, that's the way we do things on this boat, isn't it?' He looked hard at her. 'Everyone kept in the picture about what's going on?'

She grew pink and looked down at the tray. For all his 'silly ass' act, her brother could be quite astute when he chose. But she wasn't ready to share her secret yet. It was too new, too vulnerable. Besides, she'd had no time to come to terms with it herself. 'Roll up your trouser leg,' she ordered briskly. 'As soon as I've sorted you out, I have to see to Alain. But I'll join you for dinner. I haven't had the chance to find out how you got trapped in the first place.'

'OK.' He sat on the treatment table and bent his knee for Melanie to unroll the bandage. 'I promise you one thing.'

'Oh? What's that?' She lifted off the pad carefully.

'Ow! Watch it!' Derek winced as a stitch caught on the gauze. 'I won't let fame change me.' His face split in a grin, and Melanie burst out laughing as she redressed the wound.

At dawn the following morning, Luke dropped anchor in the shelter of Fort Dauphin bay. Melanie had woken early. She had slept well despite the boat's pitching and rolling on the rough sea, not doubting for one moment Luke's ability to cope with the violent conditions. But her mind had been too busy for further sleep, and after a few minutes tossing and turning she had heard the rattle of the anchor chain and got out of bed.

Slipping a sweater over her shirt and jeans against the early morning chill, she had gone on deck. The heavy black clouds, having shed their burden of rain, had raced

away. The sky was clear, the silver grey of dawn turning
to aquamarine as the first blush of sunrise tinted the
eastern horizon. The pink became gold, then fiery yellow
as the sun's huge disc climbed out of the sea, banishing
the blurred outlines and purple shadows.

Harsh and brilliant, the tropical sun was too bright to
face, so Melanie turned away and crossed the deck to
watch instead the long swell rushing shoreward to crash
in a welter of foam on the sandy beach.

The throbbing engines were once more silent. No birds
cried. The wind had dropped completely. It was as if the
world held its breath. Then a door slammed and she
looked along the deck to see Luke coming towards her
from the bridge. Her heart leapt, but she didn't move,
waiting, uncertain.

'You're a sight for sore eyes.' He smiled, and caressing
her hair, drew her towards him and laid his cheek against
her temple. It was a greeting more tender, more subtle
than a kiss, and Melanie didn't understand the lump in
her throat as she leaned against him, feeling his breath on
her face. She blinked away the tears that trembled on her
lashes, opening her eyes very wide so that they should not
fall.

Suddenly he moved, holding her away from him, his
strong hands gripping her upper arms as he looked down
into her face. A tiny crease appeared between his brows.
Had he noticed? Would he ask? How could she explain?
But he didn't speak. The frown cleared and he raised one
hand to gently cup her cheek, caressing the flushed skin
with his thumbs. He smiled and she saw that he knew,
and understood.

'I'm going to shower and shave,' he said. 'You fetch
your swimming gear and ask François to pack us some
lunch. As soon as we've had breakfast we'll take the
inflatable and go ashore. There's at least three miles of

golden sand around this bay. I daresay we'll find a bit to suit us.'

By the time they reached the beach, surfing the rubber dinghy in on the rolling breakers, the sun was high in the sky. A breeze had sprung up and the air smelled of jasmine, vanilla and seaweed.

Wet to the thighs despite rolling up her jeans, and exhilarated by the bucking ride across the choppy bay, Melanie helped Luke haul the inflatable up the sand beyond the high water mark. They were about a mile and a half from the town on the right-hand curve of the bay, sheltered from the breeze by the high grass-covered bank.

Luke dropped the rucksack and his sandals and stripping off his shirt and rolled-up jeans to reveal his swimming trunks, shook out his towel and stretched out on his back. 'Wake me in an hour,' he said, and giving a huge yawn, closed his eyes.

Melanie stared down at him in total astonishment. Since she had first seen him on deck that morning she had been buffeted like a leaf in a gale by clamouring thoughts and worries. What would they talk about? The mission? The problems they might encounter on the next dive? Should she ask him about the cargo? Or would the conversation be confined to personal matters in the light of the relationship that was developing between them? How would she cope with a situation she longed for yet was afraid of? She had had no answers, but the questions had kept nagging at her, winding her tighter and tighter like a coiled spring.

Her gaze swept up the darkly tanned body at her feet, from the long, firmly-muscled legs, lean, narrow hips encased in black, close-fitting trunks, over his flat stomach and broad chest to his face. The clear-cut features were relaxed. The wind stirred his hair, glinting on the strands of silver at his temples. His breathing was deep and regular, and Melanie realised with a start that he was sound asleep.

Her momentary irritation was swamped by self-mocking humour. The problem of what to talk about had been neatly taken out of her hands. She felt a rush of tenderness and guilt. Of course he was tired, he had every right to be. While she had slept, he had been up on the bridge, steering the boat away from the shore to ride out the storm in the deeper, safer waters of the ocean. In the dim light he would have sat at the wheel watching the foaming crests of towering waves smashed down by sheets of torrential rain. He would have heard the wind's screaming fury as it hurled tons of black water at the pitching vessel in which five men and a woman depended for their lives on his skill and nerve, taking both completely for granted. Her tension melted away and, as comfortable as if she had been alone, she kicked off her sandals and stripped down to her bikini. Taking some grips from a pocket in her beach bag, she twisted her hair into a knot on top of her head. Then after detaching the halter strap from her green bikini top and covering all the parts of her body she could reach with sun-tan lotion, she lay back on her towel and stretched like a cat. She felt the sun soaking into her bones, soothing her nerves. She listened to the breeze sighing and whispering in the palms that topped the bank. The rhythmic thunder of the breakers grew fainter and fainter.

She woke with a start to see Luke leaning on one elbow, watching her. He had moved closer and, hot with self-consciousness, she realised he had been studying her the way she had studied him. His eyes were narrowed and a lazy smile lifted one corner of his mouth. 'Welcome back,' he murmured, and leaning over, kissed her lightly. Raising his head, he looked into her eyes. He was no longer smiling. She started to sit up, but he laid a restraining hand on her shoulder, his fingers warm and strong. Melanie knew she should move away, re-establish some distance between them, but his eyes, so clear, so piercingly blue beneath the narrowed lids, held her immobile. This time, when his lips touched hers, unable to help herself, she responded, her mouth softening, parting under his tender assault.

Luke released her and they stared at one another for a long moment, both still caught up in the unexpectedly powerful effects of the kiss. Then with a self-mocking smile, he raised one hand in a fending-off gesture and shifted backwards, widening the space between them. He propped himself up on one elbow and raked not entirely steady fingers through his thick hair.

'You haven't asked about *Buckingham*'s cargo. Don't you want to know what we're looking for?'

'Of course I do,' she cried, grateful for his self-restraint, yet at the same time conscious of a pang of yearning, quickly buried. She rolled over on to her stomach, resting her chin in the heels of her hands. 'I intended to ask you today, as a matter of fact, especially as it seems I'm the only person on board who's still in the dark.'

'Why do you think that?'

The question surprised her. 'Well, I don't know, it's just——'

'You're wrong. No one else knows. I said I'd tell them when the time came. You're the first.

She looked startled. 'I am?'

'If you felt like that, why didn't you bring it up before?' He was watching her with an intent curiosity, and she sensed her reply would answer for him more than one question. It unsettled her.

'In case you've forgotten, things have been a bit hectic lately,' she retorted. 'And anyway, I—assumed you would tell me, sooner or later.'

He leaned down. 'Assuming again, Melanie?' He shook his head. 'How often people assume they know what others are thinking and feeling, but they never actually bother to find out. Busily projecting their own reactions and emotions on to others, they're mystified and hurt when someone they think they know so well turns out to be a total stranger.' He smiled and she realised his irritation was not directed specifically at her, but at the human race.

'You're right,' she said quietly, 'but sometimes it's so difficult to know——'

'When to ask, as well as what?' he finished. 'True, but what if one or two doors slam in your face? One rejection isn't the end of the world, one blow doesn't put you down for ever. Life is for living, to be savoured to the full.' He shrugged. 'So you drop the occasional clanger, or someone turns out to be less than you thought, what the hell? As long as you've learned something, there's no harm done. The worst thing is to withdraw, to reduce life to mere existence by running scared. If you keep on trying, no one can ever say you've failed. All of which has nothing to do with the cargo.' They shared a smile, his self-deprecating, hers tentative, uncertain. Had she the courage to adopt his philosophy? It was logical and sensible and she knew in her heart he was right, but Paul had destroyed something in her, and she was still entangled in a web of fear.

'Hey, are you listening?'

She squinted up at him. 'Of course, I'm hanging on your every word.'

'Hmm,' one dark brow tilted ironically, 'well in 1600, Queen Elizabeth granted a charter to English merchants trading in India, the East India Company,' Luke began, and reaching forward picked up Melanie's bottle of sun-tan lotion. He poured some into his hand and started stroking it over the lower half of her back. 'By 1700, the company was extremely powerful.' He worked the lotion into her skin with slow, circular movements, and recovering from her initial surprise and the physical shock of his touch on her bare skin, she laid her arms flat on the towel, resting her head on them as he moved upwards to her shoulders. There was nothing tentative in his touch. His hand was warm and strong and the tips of his fingers kneaded her flesh with easy confidence. Had he asked, she would have declined, but already she could feel the knots in her neck and shoulders loosening under his expert, almost absent-minded handling. 'During the next hundred years, the British and French fought for possession of the decaying Mogul empire. The East India Company won and virtually ruled India until the British government took over after Indian troops mutinied in 1858. Am I boring you?' There was laughter in his deep voice.

Her eyes flew open and she blushed. 'No, of course not.' She flexed her shoulders. 'It feels so nice. I can never reach my own back properly.'

'Just keep still. You'll fry in this sun if you aren't protected, though you look as though you tan well.' With finger and thumb he deftly unhooked the bikini top and flicked the two ends apart.

Immediately, Melanie reared up, clutching the scrap of material to her breasts. 'Now, just a min——'

'Lie still,' he pushed her down. 'You don't want to look like a traffic crossing, do you?' He held the bottle over her back and poured out some more lotion, then setting it aside began once more to knead and massage. 'Melanie, you're supposed to be relaxing,' he said impatiently. 'This is a day off, rest and recreation, a chance to recuperate from yesterday, and I had the daft idea you'd be interested to know about the cargo.'

She turned her head towards him on the towel. 'I am, and I do. Honestly.' She gave a lopsided grin and shrugged. 'I guess I'm just not used to——'

'That's obvious. Just try to remember, this native is friendly. OK?'

She nodded and surrendered herself to a growing contentment.

'Now where had I got to? Oh yes. A prince of one of the Indian states had removed a quantity of jewels from his father's palace and was trying, with the aid of *Buckingham*'s captain, to smuggle them out of India, intending to follow later when a scapegoat had been executed for the crime, "proving" *him* innocent. However, someone talked and the Prince was arrested. After trying to brazen it out he accused Captain Elliot of stealing the jewels. Elliot knew he had no chance of proving he was an innocent dupe in the plan, an admission which would have reflected badly on the company, so before his ship could be impounded, he sneaked out under cover of darkness and sailed for home, intending to make a full statement when he reached England. As you know, he never made it.' His hand rested, still, in the small of her back.

'But the jewels—why did he sail with them on board? Why not simply return them to their rightful owner?'

'That presented a slight problem as, after the Prince's rather frenzied denunciation, he didn't know who the rightful owner was.'

'How did Lucas Avery find out about all this?'

'It's quite possible he was deliberately informed by a rival of Elliot's, with an eye to splitting the cargo between them.'

Melanie looked up at him, shocked. 'An East India Company Captain sell a colleague to a gang of pirates?'

'Business was business,' Luke said flatly. 'There's documented evidence proving that a pirate named John Plantain settled in Ranter Bay on the island of St Mary in 1720, and in 1722 he was trading silks, diamonds and gold with British naval vessels who were fully aware the goods had been plundered.'

Melanie was lost for words, but she didn't have long to dwell on it, for Luke reached over and after dropping a quick kiss on her right shoulder blade, refastened her bikini top and sat up.

'I'm famished! Let's see what François has provided.'

While they ate, Luke told her of the different oceans he had worked in. 'I don't think I've been home more than a half a dozen times in the past five years.'

'Where's home?' asked Melanie.

'Berkshire. When I left California I bought myself a place just outside Mapledurham.'

'Good grief,' she spluttered, 'we're practically neighbours! I was born in Maidenhead. My father's still in practice there.'

'No mother?'

She shook her head. 'She died when we were twelve. She went into hospital for a minor operation and something went wrong with the anaesthetic. She never came round.'

Luke took her hand and pressed it. 'At least you had a brother, and your father.' He spoke comfortingly, but something in his tone jarred. He was gazing out over the bay, idly swirling the glass of iced fruit juice in his other hand.

Sympathy welled up. 'You too?'

'Car smash. Dad was killed outright, Mother lasted a week. There was no other family. I was fifteen. I've been on the move ever since. Boarding school, holidays either at home or abroad with various sets of relatives, university in England and the States.' He turned his head towards her. 'Then about five years ago I got the urge to put down some roots, establish a permanent base.'

He's married. The thought hit her like a savage blow and she felt suddenly sick and hollow. With difficulty she swallowed the piece of pineapple she was chewing. 'Any particular reason?' she asked lightly, mentally preparing herself, even as she wondered why it should hurt so much.

'I'm thirty-five years old,' he said, 'isn't that reason enough?' But the gleam in his eye told her he had missed nothing.

'What's it like, your house?' She prayed her flush didn't show in the bright sunlight.

'Just a thatched cottage. But it stands on the side of a hill in five acres of beechwoods.'

Melanie closed her eyes, picturing the cool green shade in summer and the crisp carpet of gold, crimson and brown on an autumn day. 'It must be lovely.'

'It is. A couple from the village keep an eye on it for me. The husband looks after the garden and his wife lights a fire once in a while to keep the place aired.' He smiled at some memory.

'How can you bear to have a home like that and be away so long?' Her tone was wistful and she thought of the rambling old rectory she and Derek had been brought up in by her father's sister. So much of it unused, the rooms cold and shrouded in dust sheets. But her father had refused to move, even after she and Derek had left for university, living mostly in the huge kitchen. He had converted one of the downstairs rooms into a surgery, another into a waiting room. So whenever she or her brother went back, news of their return was around the village almost before they set foot in the house, spread by the patients, none of whom wanted him to move while constantly warning her that the place was too much for him.

He still held her hand, his fingers loosely entwined with hers. 'I love the sea, I love the work I do,' he said, adding softly, almost as an afterthought, 'most of the time. I'm not married, so there isn't the same urgency to go back. But I know it's there, waiting for me, for the right time,' he swallowed the last of his fruit juice, 'and the right woman.'

The sun was sinking towards the mountains. There was a haze in the air and the regular afternoon rain clouds loomed. Luke released her hand and rose to his feet. 'Come on, let's get back to the boat before we get another soaking.' Rolling his jeans and shirt in his towel, he began to pack the rucksack.

Melanie tried to stifle a pang of regret as she quickly dressed. It had been a lovely day. All good things had to end some time, but this had gone so very fast.

'I've got an idea!' Luke yelled above the roar of the outboard as the inflatable bounced over the waves towards the boat. 'Much as I enjoy the company of my crew at dinner, I'd like you to myself for once. What do you say to a meal at the hotel tonight?'

Melanie could hardly contain her delight. 'I'd love it!' she shouted back, then blinked and wiped the shower of spray from her face with the back of her hand. 'Just one tiny problem——'

'Don't worry, I'll bring the boat in alongside the jetty.'

Fresh and cool from her shower, Melanie was sitting on the bed in bra and pants of white cotton lace, drying her hair, when Luke walked in clad only in a towel.

He raised both hands as she swung round, startled. 'I knocked, I swear.' His eyes darkened as they flickered over her slender body, her skin golden against the brief garments. 'You obviously can't hear over that thing,' he indicated the hair-dryer and Melanie switched it off. 'I need some clothes.' He opened the wardrobe. She wondered whether to pull the terrycloth robe around her, but logic reminded her she was wearing as much as she had on the beach. Luke tossed a beige safari shirt and matching trousers on the bed.

This is ridiculous, Melanie thought. To an outsider, it would appear we've been living together for years. She felt a little thrill of satisfaction, then flushed at her own temerity.

'Your brother caught me as I was coming into the day cabin,' he said, rummaging in a drawer and pulling out clean underpants. 'He wants to buy us a celebration drink at the hotel this evening, and I accepted.'

Melanie brushed her hair vigorously, hoping to hide her disappointment. 'That will be nice. What are we celebrating?'

He shut the drawer and picking up the shirt and trousers went to the door. 'Being alive? However, I made it quite clear that you and I are dining alone.' He raised one dark brow. 'Any objections?'

She smiled shyly. 'None at all.'

Twenty minutes later she emerged. Luke had his back to her and was flicking over the pages of the log on his desk. Her heart did a peculiar little skip. The crisply ironed safari suit made him appear taller and darker and he looked devastatingly handsome.

Melanie was as nervous as a girl on her first date, and pulled the door closed with a soft click. He turned at the sound and she felt her colour rise as with slow deliberation, he examined her from head to toe.

For coolness she had swept her hair up into a soft chignon, secured with combs. Lashings of moisturiser had given her skin an opalescent sheen, and her eyes, enhanced by gold shadow, seemed larger than usual. His gaze lingered on her mouth, given a ripe fullness by the rose lip-gloss.

Her camisole top was of white broderie anglaise, tucked into a matching tiered skirt. A lacy shawl of rose-pink angora hung over one arm. Gold and white sandals and a small white purse completed her outfit.

He came towards her and she smelled the masculine

fragrance of his aftershave. He bent his head, and the touch of his lips below her ear sent a delicious shiver down her spine. Straightening up, he looked into her eyes. 'You're beautiful,' he said softly, and drawing her arm through his, led her out of the cabin and along the passage. 'Though I have to admit I did rather fancy the outfit,' he added a few moments later.

Puzzled, Melanie glanced up. 'What other outfit?'

He helped her up the stairs. 'The one under your dress,' he murmured as they emerged on deck.

She glanced at him, then started to laugh.

Derek turned from his contemplation of the fast-fading sunset. In a blue short-sleeved shirt over stone-coloured trousers, he looked scrubbed and shining. 'What's the joke? Or is it private?' he grinned with heavy innuendo.

'No joke,' Luke said calmly. 'I was simply admiring your sister's taste in—' he hesitated and Melanie caught her breath, '—clothes,' he finished blandly, and she carefully and deliberately stepped back on to his toe. He didn't flinch.

'Oh,' grunted Derek, vaguely disappointed.

The rain-cooled air was heavy with the scent of jasmine and cloves as they walked the short distance from the jetty to the hotel. The sky was a glittering carpet of stars and a waning moon hung low over the water, tipping the breaking waves with silver as they shushed on to the beach.

With her arm through Luke's, her fingers resting on the corded muscles, Melanie had never known such contentment.

In the tiny bar, Derek ordered the first round, and as he would be unable to dive until his leg had healed, requested a Bacardi and lime, with childlike relish. Luke and Melanie stuck to fruit juice and listened as Derek regaled them with hair-raising stories about films he had made for the Wildlife Unit. The stories were genuinely amusing, and they had both laughed, but their eyes kept meeting and sliding away only to meet again seconds later.

Melanie hadn't taken much notice of the two men at the corner table until the girl walked in, her black, low-necked sheath emphasising her creamy skin and voluptuous curves. Her auburn hair cascaded down her back in tawny waves and her make-up was bold and dramatic, yet beneath the glamorous façade, Melanie sensed anxiety. But the impression was fleeting and she quickly forgot it. She sat down with the two men, and Derek, half-way through a story, couldn't take his eyes off her.

'She's got company, Derek,' Luke warned quickly, 'and they don't look the sort who'd be willing to share.'

One of the men snapped his fingers and a waiter immediately placed a tray of drinks on the table, removing the men's empty glasses. The girl seemed to be arguing with them, but there were no raised voices; she was quiet, almost desperate. One placed a drink in front of her. She pushed it away, but he simply pushed it back, murmuring quietly as the other took a folded paper out of his pocket and laid it on the table. She stared at it, then after a few moments picked up the drink, and gripping the glass so tightly her knuckles gleamed white in the dim light, she swallowed the amber liquid in three gulps, shuddering as she put the glass down. Then she got up and walked out of the bar, staring straight ahead of her, ignoring Derek's 'Hi there,' as she passed him. The man with the paper returned it to his inside pocket and after finishing their drinks they too left, talking quietly to one another. As they passed Melanie heard one say the name Pierre, and something about a government department, but the French was too heavily accented to follow. She turned to Luke. He was staring after the men, his face like granite.

'What is it?' An icy finger trailed down her spine.

He looked at her as though he'd forgotten she was there. 'Nothing,' he said abruptly, then with a visible effort he relaxed and shrugged. 'I don't like to see a woman scared even if she is, as my great-aunt used to say, no better than she should be.'

Derek stood up. 'Time I was off, as it's perfectly clear I'm not invited to stay for dinner. I think I'll see what other night-life this metropolis has to offer. Have fun.' Waving over his shoulder, he limped out.

'He's going after her.' Melanie's concern showed on her face.

'He's old enough to take care of himself,' Luke replied calmly.

'But those men——'

'He won't find her unless she intends him to, in which case she will have already taken them into account. Now, shall we order?'

The lobster was succulent, the salad crisp and the sorbet cool and refreshing, and as Luke talked of the countries he had worked in, and about buying the boat, Melanie let the incident slip from her mind. She was falling deeper and deeper under Luke's spell. He asked her opinions and listened when she gave them. He spoke of his youth, of his loneliness among the crowds at school and university. And she, who had missed a mother's comfort and guidance more acutely than her brother, knew and understood. He made her rock with laughter over his dealings with estate agents during his search for a house, and as they strolled back to the jetty it seemed perfectly natural that his arm should be around her and her head rest so comfortably on his shoulder.

They entered the day cabin and he closed the door. Melanie's heart began to thud against her ribs as, instead of switching on the main light, he pressed the button on the desk lamp, leaving the rest of the cabin in soft shadow.

She swallowed. 'It—it's been a wonderful evening, Luke.'

Silently he lifted the lacy shawl from her shoulders, the purse from her unprotesting hands, and laid both on the desk, then taking her hands in his he raised them in turn to his lips. His eyes never left hers as he released her hands and, tenderly cupping her face, bent his head to take possession of her mouth. Her arms crept around his waist and as her lips parted under the pressure of his, Melanie gave a tiny inarticulate moan as her body was flooded with sweet warmth.

Her skin burned as his fingers slid lightly over her bare shoulders and down her back. He groaned softly and crushed her against him, his mouth hot and demanding. She could feel passion rising in him and a fine trembling shook her as his body grew taut against hers. Her head was spinning, but as his hand came round to cup her breast, fragments of the nightmare flashed through her brain.

She panicked and tore her mouth free. 'No!' she gasped, dragging in lungfuls of air. 'No, don't.'

He too was shaking as he stared down at her, his eyes glittering feverishly. The lower half of her body was still hard against him, his arm unyielding as a steel hawser. He tensed, and a treacherous weakness rippled through her, but fear, and the memory of pain, was too strong. 'Please,' tears were streaming down her cheeks, 'I can't. let me go!'

He released her at once, steadying her as she staggered. 'Mel, I'm sorry,' his voice was hoarse. 'I didn't mean—Lord, I'm a clumsy bastard. Did I hurt you?'

She shook her head, wiping her face with the flat of her hand. He passed her his handkerchief. 'I've wanted to kiss you since that first moment on the beach when you sprang to your brother's defence.' He jammed both hands into his pockets as the urge to hold her threatened to overpower him. 'You were like a tigress protecting her cub. Dammit, Melanie,' his voice roughened, 'you've come to mean so much to me.'

'Don't,' she begged, 'you mustn't—I'm not——' and turned away as scalding tears brimmed once more. How could she bear it?

Her heart longed for his love, and her body quivered and sang at his touch. But her mind recoiled in horror, locked in the memory of that terrible night, the drunken brutal violation she was forced to relive in her nightmares.

He caught her arm, letting go at once as she flinched. His breath was hot on her shoulder and she could feel him battling against the desire to touch her. 'What did I do?' he rasped. 'What happened, what scared you?'

Paul, she screamed in silent anguish, Paul happened. She looked over her shoulder at him, agonised. 'I—I—it's too soon,' she whispered, and ran to her cabin.

CHAPTER EIGHT

AFTER a restless, dream-filled night, Melanie woke to the throbbing hum of the boat's engines. She forced herself to think rationally. If they were returning to the wreck site, the sea must have abated sufficiently to resume diving. With Derek injured she would have to take over as photographer. Though she welcomed the extra work, which would keep her fully stretched, she would be forced even more into Luke's company.

Her body quivered as she relived his kiss and the startling thrill of arousal. She saw again the fever of desire in his eyes, felt the urgency in his body and her own delicious response.

She swung her legs out of bed and buried her head in her hands. Why? Why did these memories haunt and torment her? The discovery of joy in Luke's arms had been smothered by choking, agonising fear. Would she ever conquer it? Or had Paul destroyed for ever her ability to love and be loved?

She sat up, pushing her tumbled hair back from her damp forehead. For so long she had been completely numb, but now her protective shell was cracked and falling apart. In less than a week Luke Avery had breached her defences and was subjecting her to the tortures of physical and emotional reawakening. Could she, should she trust him? She wanted to, so much, but . . .

A door slammed and she jumped. For a moment she thought it was the outer door to the passage, but the raised voices came through the bulkhead from Derek's cabin. Glad to be delivered from her own thoughts, and

131

wondering what was going on, Melanie washed and dressed quickly. The voices subsided, the door slammed again and a few moments later, Luke and her brother walked into the day cabin just as she emerged.

'What else could I have done, for God's sake?' Derek was demanding, his tone a mixture of defiance and apology.

'Would you like me to leave?' Melanie said quickly. Her heart ached at the sight of the tall, dark figure.

Luke shook his head. 'No, this concerns you as well. Your brother has been busy playing Sir Galahad, and has probably blown our cover.'

'Luke, I had no choice—she was terrified! Besides, she couldn't possibly know anything. I'm the only person she's seen since—until you came in this morning.'

Melanie wrenched her thoughts from Luke and gazed at her brother in concern. 'What's Luke talking about? What's happened?'

Derek shoved both hands into his pockets. He looked tired and a stubble of fair beard was visible on his chin. 'That girl in the hotel last night, she's in trouble.'

'What sort of trouble?'

'You saw the two guys she was with? They're blackmailing her.'

'Blackmailing?' Melanie repeated in bewilderment. 'But how? I mean how do you know?'

'How do you think?' Derek exploded. 'She told me, didn't she?'

'That will do,' snapped Luke. 'You got us into this, don't start taking it out on Melanie!'

She looked at him quickly. Despite her panic-stricken rejection, her lack of explanation, he was defending her. But as he caught her eye she saw in his brief glance a determination to uncover the truth behind her behaviour. She shied away from the thought and the pain it promised.

Derek shrugged jerkily and she recognised the movement as an apology.

'I don't understand,' she looked bewildered, 'Derek, what have you got us into? Where did you meet her? And why did she tell you all this? You haven't seen her before, have you?'

He shook his head. 'When I left you both at the bar, I went out on to the verandah. She was in a corner, crying. Hell, I couldn't just ignore her!'

Melanie shot an involuntary glance at Luke. He was watching her and raised his eyebrows. She could read cynicism at her brother's naïvety, and felt her own loyalty sharply divided.

'She was scared to death,' Derek went on. 'They'd been threatening her in the bar, describing certain "accidents" that could happen if she doesn't do what they want, accidents that will scar her for life. Her name is Selena Stuart, and she's an actress and model. Her looks are her livelihood.'

Melanie was even more confused. 'But why are they threatening her? I mean, what have they got to blackmail her with?'

'They say she signed a contract to appear in a film they're making, further up the coast.'

'She's certainly got the looks for it,' Melanie allowed, 'so what's the problem?'

'Selena swears she never signed that contract. Either she was tricked into it, thinking she was signing something else, or her signature was forged. But she's got no money to pay her fare home. She thinks the men stole her bag containing all her travel documents and cash.'

'But if she's got a contract, then surely she'd be paid, so why doesn't she just make the film? She'd have some money and the men would stop threatening.'

'It's hard-core porn, Mel,' her brother said quietly. 'Would you?'

Her stomach contracted. 'Oh God!' she whispered.
She'd read of such things in the newspapers, and
wondered briefly how girls ever got themselves into such
situations, then she had turned the page and forgotten
about it. But this was someone her brother knew, and it
wasn't going to go away.

'What did you do? Where is she now?'

'Next door, in his cabin,' Luke answered bitterly. 'He
smuggled her on board last night, and didn't see fit to
inform me or anyone else. So we're on our way to try and
complete a secret mission which is reaching its most
critical point, accompanied by a total stranger.'

'OK, OK!' shouted Derek. 'You've made your point.'
He raked both hands through his sandy hair, looking
suddenly young and vulnerable. 'Dammit, she was
petrified! She's got no money, no one to turn to, and
those two gorillas are threatening to carve her up.' He
swung round and glared at Luke. 'What would you have
done?' Melanie silently echoed the question.

Luke leaned back on the desk and folded his arms.
'First of all, I would have asked myself a few questions—
I might even have mentioned them to her. Like, how, if
she had no money, she got to Fort Dauphin, and why she
chose to come here instead of returning to Tamatave or
the capital. Like, why did she appear in the bar wearing
heavy make-up and such a provocative dress, unless it
was a deliberate ploy to catch the attention of the only
unaccompanied man present. And,' he went on relentlessly, allowing Derek no chance to interrupt, 'given our
reason for being on this part of the island, and the
necessary secrecy which has surrounded our whole
operation, it might have occurred to me to wonder if I
was being set up. But then,' with a mildness that only
underlined his bitter anger, 'I suppose I have a nasty,
suspicious nature.'

It was obvious from the expressions chasing across

Derek's face that no such doubts or questions had crossed his mind. Even now, forced to recognise the possibility, he was plainly resisting the thought that he'd been duped.

Melanie too was shaken. Luke's words had put an entirely different slant on the whole situation, though, like Derek, she didn't want to believe it. She was out of her depth. 'What are you going to do?' she asked Luke. 'Perhaps we should call in the police.'

'For what purpose?'

'Well, they could protect her——'

'From what? Threats? No crime has been committed, except by her if she's left the hotel without paying her bill. Besides, if her signature is on that contract, there's nothing they can do. It would be a matter for the civil court.' He shook his head. 'No,' he said calmly, 'the police will not be informed. Their involvement at this stage of the operation would destroy months of work and endanger several people. I'll handle this my own way.'

An icy chill rippled down Melanie's spine. Luke was suddenly a stranger. She could see no trace of the man who had shared the secrets of his lonely childhood, who had kissed her with heart-aching tenderness and soul-stirring passion. The man who switched his hard stare from Derek to herself was cold, implacable, and utterly determined. There would be no police. Again, the fleeting thought assailed her; which side of the law was Luke really on?

'What *is* your way?' Derek demanded truculently, his tone suggesting Luke's idea might require discussion. Luke's brief, contemptuous glance immediately shattered that illusion, and as Derek visibly wilted, Melanie released the breath she'd been unaware of holding.

'Selena Stuart does not leave this boat until the mission is completed. She is not left alone at any time. If she's genuine she'll be grateful for our protection. If she's not, she'll have no opportunity to use the radio or signal anyone without one of us knowing. She's all yours, Derek.' Luke's smile did not reach his eyes. 'She'll sleep in your cabin. You might even get her to help process the films. Make sure you keep her out of sight until lunchtime—I want time to tell Callum and the others what's happened. Did she bring anything with her? A change of clothes?'

Derek shook his head. 'She wouldn't go back into the hotel. She was afraid if the men saw her with me——' His voice trailed off, then his face brightened. 'Surely that proves she's innocent,' he cried. 'She was so desperate to get away, she just left everything. No girl would willingly abandon all her personal belongings.'

'Innocent or guilty, if it got her where she wanted to go, she might well consider the sacrifice worthwhile,' Luke replied.

'Well, she can't spend the next week in that black dress,' Melanie pointed out. 'I can lend her a shirt, but——' she looked down at her own slender figure, 'I don't think my trousers would be much use.'

'Mel, you're a doll,' Derek grinned weakly, plainly relieved at the change of subject. 'I'll find some shorts or a pair of jeans for her.'

'You can ask Herbie for an extra toothbrush and so on,' Luke put in unexpectedly, and glancing at him, Melanie realised it was her gesture which had prompted his. He beckoned her and opened the door. 'Derek, if anything fouls up the rest of this job, anything that can be traced to the girl, I shall hold you personally responsible.' His voice was very quiet. 'And I warn you, if that happens——'

'There's no need for threats, Luke,' Derek was struggling to maintain a dignified front, but his grand gesture had fallen to pieces in front of him, and though he tried to hide it, he was worried.

'Breakfast, Melanie,' ordered Luke, but the gleam in his eyes belied his curtness. 'Then re-charge the cylinders, we'll do a reconnaissance dive at ten.'

'Will you want photographs?' She kept her voice level though her heart thumped unevenly.

He thought for a moment. 'Bring the stills camera, just in case.'

'Mel?' Derek scratched his ear. 'The—er—shirt?'

Luke shook his head and walked out as Melanie hurried back into her cabin and opening a drawer, took out a yellow, sleeveless T-shirt and a short-sleeved blouse of pale green cotton, neither of which she had worn.

'It's not what he thinks,' muttered Derek, 'Selena's not like that.'

'For all our sakes I hope you're right.' She pushed the garments into her brother's hand. 'I'll call for the camera after breakfast.'

'Mel!' he called after her as she started down the passage. She looked enquiringly over her shoulder. 'Watch yourself—not all sharks live in the sea!' Leaving her staring after him, he went into his cabin and closed the door.

Her brother's remark bothered her all through a breakfast punctuated by François, Gauloise glowing fiercely, trying to find out what the stowaway looked like and what Melanie knew about her.

'Honestly, François, I only saw her for a few minutes and the lights were dim. All I remember is that she has long auburn hair——'

'What is zis owburn?' he interrupted, frowning.

'Sort of reddish gold. She had pale skin and was wearing a black dress.'

'And she is pretty, yes?' he demanded, the coffee pot poised over her cup, and Melanie wondered whether if she said no, he would refuse to pour. She recalled the green eyeshadow and heavy eye-liner; the vivid slash of mouth.

'I think perhaps striking, rather than pretty. Anyway, you'll see for yourself when she comes to meals.'

'Ha,' François snorted, closing one eye against the curling smoke, 'I sink 'ell will freeze before ze Capitaine welcome 'er at zis table.' He waddled out.

When she went to collect the camera, Derek wanted her to stay and meet Selena. 'She's just getting changed. She was ever so grateful for the shirts. Honestly, Mel, she's nothing like the picture Luke's trying to paint, you'll see.'

His face fell when she said she couldn't, and she saw that he desperately wanted reassurance, that if she met and liked Selena, his actions would be vindicated. She was torn; she loved her brother and knew that he had acted out of kindness, if too hastily. But he was laying an unfair responsibility on her and she already had too many pressing problems of her own.

'I wish I could, Derek, but I'm already late. One of the relief valves on the compressor kept sticking. Luke will be waiting, and I——'

'And that would never do,' he cut in pettishly. 'When Luke says jump, we all leap up and down, or else.'

'That's enough!' Melanie's cheeks flushed angrily. 'This isn't a pleasure cruise. You're being paid, remember? It isn't Luke's fault, or mine, that we're in this mess, so don't try shifting the blame—and while we're at it, I'm having to do your work as well as my own, *and* we're limited to certain stages of the tide for diving.'

'I see.' His grin was twisted. 'Well, it's pretty obvious whose side you're on. Who said blood was thicker than water?' He thrust the camera into her hands and retreated into the cabin.

'Derek, wait,' Melanie took a step forward, 'you've got it all wrong, I wasn't——' The door closed in her face.

She stared at the varnished wood for a few seconds, then turned away and went down to the diving room.

Luke, already in his wetsuit, was sitting on the bench, rubbing saliva over the inside of his mask to prevent the faceplate misting. As he glanced up all her resentment at Derek's unfairness, her confusion over her reactions to Luke, the emotional upheaval she was undergoing and the added stress of uncertainty over this new threat to the mission, solidified into a churning lump in her stomach. Just one word, she challenged him silently, one comment about Derek's stupidity, or her being late, or last night and she would blow the roof off the cabin!

'Callum says you changed the filter in the compressor,' he remarked.

'Yes,' she said tightly, ready to defend her action.

'I thought it must be time. Callum does tend to try and squeeze one more hour's use out of them. How many have we got left?'

'Two.'

He put the mask to one side, stood up and slipped his arms into the cylinder harness. 'I've tried Activated Alumina and Silica Gel filters in that compressor, and they're both quite effective. Which do you use at the Institute?'

As she realised there was no criticism implied, Melanie allowed herself to relax. She laid the camera on the bench and taking her suit off the hanger, went behind the rack to change. 'Neither. We used to use Silica Gel because it changes colour when it becomes saturated with water, which makes it easy to tell when the filter needs changing. But now we use Molecular Sieve. As it removes both water vapour and oil mist, it's extremely efficient, but it's also more expensive than either of the others.'

'Even so, if it is more efficient it could be worth trying,' Luke said. 'You nearly ready?'

She zipped up her jacket and came out from behind the
rack. He held her harness ready and she turned her back
to put her arms through the straps.

'Better now?' he asked softly. There was a smile in his
voice and she knew at once he had recognised the
pressure within her and his talk of filters had been a
deliberate ploy to steer her thoughts away from everything but the dive ahead. He had succeeded. She nodded,
and moved away, clipping the buckle closed. But he
caught her arm and gently pulled her back. 'You've
forgotten something.'

She looked up at him, reading the mild reproof on his
rugged features, a frown creasing his forehead.

'Equipment check,' he reminded her.

'We both know it's not necessary.' She tried to ease
away. Being so close to him only stirred up all her
confusion.

He placed his hands on her shoulders. 'Melanie, listen
to me.' His voice was deep and quiet as he looked into her
eyes. 'Whatever problems you and I still have to sort
out——' he paused and her heart lurched; he was clearly
reminding her of her flight last night, and its cause,
'when we dive in a few minutes we will be totally
dependent on each other, not only to complete this job,
but for our very lives. Having scented blood the sharks
will be more than just curious. The Captain's stateroom
is littered with debris and a highly dangerous place in
which to work. Time is more precious than ever. The
hazards we're facing are considerable, so all the more
reason for not taking the smallest *unnecessary* risk. I'm
damn sure all my gear is complete and functioning, it's
second nature for me to check it after each dive. I've seen
you do the same, but we've both got a lot on our minds,
we could miss something.' His grip tightened. 'Look,
what I'm trying to say is that while we're on that wreck
we have to trust each other one hundred per cent, no

reservations. Everything else must take second place, understand?'

'Yes,' she whispered.

He touched her face. 'It's not all one-sided, you know,' he grated, and turned her round to examine the demand valves on her cylinders. Then he quickly checked her weight belt, straps and buckles. Cheeks aflame, trying and failing to ignore the electricity that almost crackled between them, Melanie did the same for him, then without speaking they both turned away to pick up masks, fins and torches. Melanie scooped up the camera.

The orange marker buoy bobbed brightly on the choppy water. 'It's a blessing the storm didna' take that.' Billo indicated it, handing Melanie the camera as she stood on the ladder.

'How could it?' she said softly. 'When sir ties a knot, it stays tied.'

Billo's eyebrows climbed. She blushed, quickly lowering her head to fit her mouthpiece. Holding the camera close, she placed her other hand over her mask and stepped back into the water where Luke waited to fasten the buddy-line around her wrist.

Billo watched, grinning. So much for secrecy, she thought. There didn't appear to be any resentment among the crew. In fact, since her dive on the day of the storm, she had been aware of a subtle but definite change. Where before she had been an outsider, accepted politely, but on sufferance, now she was one of them and they treated her as such, while maintaining a lively if discreet curiosity about her relationship with Luke.

She followed him down, blanking off all thoughts, keeping a careful lookout for sharks. They had sprayed each other with repellent just before entering the water, and both carried several canisters clipped to their weight belts. But so far there was no sign of the sinuous grey shapes.

As they approached the wreck, alarm bells started
ringing in Melanie's head. It looked different. She finned
alongside Luke, grabbed his arm and pointed, shaking
her head. He understood at once and had obviously seen
something more, for he gestured towards the sloping
edge of the fore-reef ahead of the bow. Melanie looked,
and even as her brain was assessing the significance of
the wider gap and the newly revealed patch of coral,
scraped clean of other marine growth, she raised the
camera, and capturing each change from a different
angle, took picture after picture. When she had finished,
Luke beckoned and she followed him down to the keel.
The change of angle had tilted the boat more on to its
side, and moved it round. It now lay directly in the path
of the tidal stream funnelling through a gap in the reef.
She felt herself caught in the powerful flow, then buffeted
by the turbulent water swirling in and out through the
gash in the hull. If it hadn't been for Luke's hold on the
buddy-line she would have been sucked down into the
gaping hole.

Kicking hard, she finned upward, out of the current.
Luke pointed towards the surface and they went up
together. She hung on to the ladder, spitting out her
mouthpiece, while he passed the camera up to Billo, then
rejoined her.

Her heart was thumping and the adrenalin surged as
her nervous system responded to the added danger. 'I
don't suppose we could try to hold the wreck in place
with ropes up to the boat, could we? Maybe use the
engines?'

Luke shook his head. 'I daren't risk it. there's a
permanent swell and if the wreck moved without
warning, the boat would be swamped before we could cut
the lines.'

Melanie was thinking hard. She shook her head.
'There are no outcrops or fissures on that area of the reef,

nothing to which we could anchor the wreck.' They bobbed in the water, facing one another, still linked by the rope looped around their wrists, both holding the ladder with their free hands.

Luke reached for the buddy-line. 'I'm going alone, Melanie, it's too——'

'No,' she cut in, grabbing his hand to prevent him unclipping the rope. 'You can't do it by yourself. Besides, you can't quote rules and regulations at me and then go and break the most important one yourself. If you're going, I'm going with you, you'll need my help. Anyway,' she went on quickly, giving him no chance to speak, 'the tide is on the rise again now. That flow through the gully is pretty powerful and should be strong enough to hold the wreck where it is on the reef.'

'But the ebb tides——' Behind the mask his eyes mirrored the conflict raging in him.

'Let's not worry about those until we have to. Right now we've got fifty minutes on a rising tide. Let's use it.'

She watched as he weighed up the risks, and wished she felt as confident as she sounded. The violent storm and low spring tides had combined to shift the wreck. Those same conditions had probably occurred several times over the centuries and each time the wreck would have turned a fraction more, slipped a bit further down the slanting reef, until it was now poised like the crouched figure of a skier at the crest of a slope. But beyond the crippled ship there was no gentle incline, just a few feet of growth-encrusted coral, then a precipitous drop into the inky depths of the Indian Ocean.

Yet the idea of waiting, safe and dry, on board Luke's boat while he went into the shifting wreck alone was unthinkable. If anything happened, if he got trapped and couldn't get out—no, she had to go, he needed her there. It was a matter of simple choice, and she would rather take the chance of dying with him than living without

him. She stared at the man less than two feet away from
her, her vision distorted by the water on her mask. *Oh
God, I love him so much.* The shattering realisation
loosened her grip on the ladder. A wave broke in her face
and she swallowed a mouthful of water. *Why now?* she
cried silently. *The first time in my life I fall in love and I
have to do it now, when either or both of us could be
killed.* She knew then it was the danger they were facing
that had torn aside all her doubt and confusion. It hadn't
solved any of the problems, but there was nothing like
staring death in the face for the second time in a few days
to sort out priorities.

'Are you all right?' Behind the faceplate, his eyes were
concerned. She nodded, not trusting herself to speak for a
moment. The concern deepened to anxiety. 'Melanie, I
can't let you——'

'Luke, are you prepared to abandon the mission?' She
kept her voice low, not wanting Billo to hear, afraid he
would misinterpret the question and her reason for
asking it. She already knew the answer.

'I can't,' he said simply. 'Not until there's literally no
chance of success.'

'And while the wreck is on the reef, we still have a
chance, don't we?' Her eyes, stripped of pretence and
evasion, held his, committing herself to him, to the
mission which meant so much to him. She saw him
wavering. 'So let's stop wasting time and get on with the
job.'

He took her hand and the intensity of his gaze,
declaring his gratitude and admiration more clearly than
any words, brought a sudden wild beat to her heart. He
pressed her fingers to his lips. Releasing her long enough
to adjust their breathing gear, his eyes never leaving hers,
Luke took her hand again and they dived once more.

They moved with great care in the hull, trying to create
as little turbulence as possible. Finally they reached the

Captain's stateroom.

Luke pulled the buddy-line taut to keep her close and drew her up to the low ceiling. They touched nothing, but shone their torches in wide regular sweeps over the heaped and broken furniture.

Melanie had to fight a growing urge to scrabble through the smashed cupboards and half-open drawers to find the small brass-bound chest Luke had described, and get out as fast as she could. The minutes were ticking inexorably away. If they didn't find it this time, they would have to come down again, and with each dive the danger was a thousand times greater.

Her gaze flickered over the mess and the shadows moved, leaping and changing as the torch beam swung. It would take hours to search every nook and cranny, and moving the heavy pieces could alter the balance of the wreck. She refused to think further.

The walls seemed to be closing in on her and for a fleeting moment she wondered, quite coolly, if she was going to succumb to claustrophobia, Luke grasped her hand. One hundred per cent trust, he'd said. Her fingers tightened on his and she fought down her panic, concentrating on breathing slowly and evenly.

He seemed to be doing nothing, just hanging in the water examining every part of the cabin with the powerful torch. They didn't have much longer. The beam of light returned yet again to a long and heavy-looking sideboard, lying at the far end of the cabin. It had fallen forward and partially crushed a leather-covered chair. Luke tugged her gently towards it. The glass in the row of narrow stern windows had long disappeared and fish swam in and out through the weed- and barnacle-crusted frames. The gaps were too narrow for anything larger than a grouper. But as Melanie glanced out into the clear, sunlit water, as if through the bars of a cage, dark shapes circled at the limit of her vision. Their slow, patient patrol held a menace that dried her throat.

She shone her torch down and recoiled as the light fell
on the crumpled skeleton trapped half-way under the
sideboard, the jaws gaping wide, still locked in a final
agony. Shreds of cloth with brass buttons attached clung
to the upper ribs. It had to be Captain Elliot. He must
have been kneeling to reach into one of the cupboards
when the storm triumphed and tons of water burst into
the cabin, smashing the lighter furniture to matchwood
and tumbling the heavier items with irresistible force.

Now Melanie understood Luke's apparent inaction.
Instead of starting an immediate search, he had, using
calculated guesswork, been deducing the most likely
hiding place for the chest. After the Prince's betrayal, the
Captain would have trusted no one; he would have kept
the jewels under lock and key in a place only he had
access to. Luke had seen the skeleton before she had and
knew that only when Captain Elliot realised the ship was
doomed would he have tried to retrieve them from their
hiding place in the desperate hope of somehow saving
them and himself. But it had been too late. Melanie
shuddered. Perhaps his fate had been sealed from the
moment he agreed to help the Prince.

Jerked out of her thoughts by Luke's tug on the line,
she followed his example and laid her torch on the floor,
its beam directed on to the sideboard. She tried to avoid
looking at the skull, its expression changed by the
torchlight to mocking laughter. She checked her watch
again. They were very close to their time limit. She
signalled Luke and tapped her watch, and he nodded and
pointed to the sideboard. As he pulled and she pushed
they tried to lift it, but it would not move. They tried once
more, air bubbles streaming up in a silvery explosion as
they strained.

Luke shook his head and motioned her back, then lay
on the floor and reached in alongside the remains of

Captain Elliot. His quick nod and thumbs-up told Melanie the door was open. But could he reach the chest? And could he get it out?

She looked at her watch. There were only minutes to go. If they ran over they would need time in the recompression chamber again, which for Luke would be highly dangerous, so soon after his last spell. Pulling hard on the buddy-line, she pointed urgently upwards. She could see the agony of indecision in his eyes. She pushed him aside and tried to wriggle in under the sideboard, but though she got further than him her cylinders jammed against the top edge. She hit the quick release buckle and shrugged out of the harness, keeping the mouthpiece gripped firmly between her teeth. Luke held the cylinders, coming in as close as he could as she squirmed under the tilted sideboard and manoeuvred both arms inside the cupboard. Her fingers touched something slimy and she swallowed, biting hard on the mouthpiece. Then at last she felt the rounded shape and metal strips of the chest top. Trying not to fumble, her fingers all thumbs, she worked it off the shelf and twisted it round to get it out of the half-open door. She had done it! She wriggled out, clutching the chest, and Luke reached down to help her when a strange ripple ran through the water. His hand clamped on her arm, biting painfully into the flesh as he hauled her up, and in that split second Melanie noticed all the fish had gone.

CHAPTER NINE

LUKE pointed to his own mouthpiece, then grasped hers. Melanie knew at once what he intended. She took a deep breath and, without hesitation, placed her life in his hands. He pulled the mouthpiece free and let the cylinders fall, then unclipped her weight belt. Holding tightly to his hand, releasing air a little at a time in a stream of silvery bubbles, she finned swiftly after him. There was no time to worry about turbulence. The wreck was moving and they were still inside it. Her heart hammered a deafening tattoo in her ears as she breathed out the remaining air. Her lungs began to burn and the urge to inhale was overpowering.

She tugged frantically at Luke's hand. Pulling her against him, he took the valve out of his mouth and helped her put it in hers. Blackness sang in her head as she sucked gratefully at the air, barely conscious of the moment they actually shot from the hatchway into the limpid ocean. But when she realised, she felt almost sick with relief and after another deep breath, passed the mouthpiece back to Luke.

The sense of danger persisted and she turned her head quickly. But if the sharks were about they were keeping their distance. Glimpsing the wreck as she looked down, it seemed to her to be shuddering. The force of the tidal stream was loosening and lifting it from the reef. On the next ebb it would be sucked over the edge and its final resting place would put Captain Elliot and what remained of his crew beyond the reach of any man. She clutched the casket so tightly it hurt.

Moments later she was heaved up the ladder by Billo

and Callum. Reaction was setting in and she shook uncontrollably as they removed her fins. 'W-we g-got it.' She tried to grin at the men.

'Aye, lass.' Callum patted her shoulder with clumsy affection. 'Ye did that.'

Luke had shed his gear and suit in record time and clad in his black shorts, gently prised the chest from Melanie's grasp and thrust it at Callum. 'Look after that,' he growled, and half-pushed, half-carried her down the steps and straight past the diving room.

'I—I'm all right,' she kept saying, but the words wouldn't come out properly, and her jaws ached from clamping them together to try and stop her teeth chattering.

Kicking the door of the day cabin shut, Luke hustled her through to the sleeping cabin. 'Get that suit off,' he ordered, and went out again. Melanie could hear him rubbing himself dry and struggled with the zip, but her fingers shook so much she couldn't grip it.

He strode back in, his hair tousled and his wet shorts replaced by the towel now wrapped around his waist. Shaking his head impatiently, he reached for the neck of her jacket.

'I—I c-can manage,' she resisted feebly, but with one swift downward sweep, the jacket parted and he peeled it off. Dropping it on the floor as Melanie made vain attempts to keep him away with one hand and cover herself with the other, he grabbed her terry cloth robe from the end of the bed and manoeuvred her arms into it. As she clutched it around her, her teeth clicking like castanets, he pushed her down on to the bed and hooking his fingers into the waistband of the Neoprene trousers, stripped them off and tossed them on to the crumpled jacket.

'H-hey!' she gasped, but ignoring her protest, he hauled her upright and began to rub her arms and back through the towelling robe with a roughness that made her wince. After a few moments her shivers eased, and resting her forehead against his shoulder she surrendered herself to the bliss of having someone take care of her, and to the glowing warmth created partly by the friction rub, and partly by the realisation that they had done it. They had actually recovered the chest and got out safely. But it had been awfully close. She closed her eyes. He had not spoken one friendly or congratulatory word to her since they had been helped aboard. Even Callum's shock as he realised they had been sharing an air supply, quickly masked by a laconic, 'Cuttin' it fine again, ah see,' had been met only with, 'The wreck's going.'

'Are you angry, Luke?' Her question was muffled, but the sudden stillness of his hands on her back told her he'd heard.

'Angry?' His voice was rough and tightly controlled, as though he could barely contain the conflict seething within him. His arms tightened around her, crushing her against him, forcing her head back. 'I should never have listened to you.' His face was harsh. 'That chest has claimed too many lives. It could have taken yours—but no more, you'll never dive with me again.'

Impulsively she reached up and caught his head between her hands. 'No,' she cried, 'don't say that! I knew what I was doing. I couldn't have let you go alone. The waiting, not knowing if you—I couldn't have borne it!'

His expression softened as first bewilderment, then comprehension dawned in his eyes. She looked down quickly, releasing his face, her hands falling to his shoulders as hot colour flooded her face. She tried to turn away, but his arms tightened. 'Melanie?'

'Regulations,' she said wildly, 'you must never dive alone, especially on a wreck.' Her voice was husky, forced from a throat as dry as paper. She hadn't meant to

let it slip, at least not yet. 'Anyway,' she stumbled on, 'I
had to be there—part of the job, I mean it's what I'm
being paid for, isn't it?' Luke's mouth covered hers,
stopping the disjointed flow of words.

The warm pressure of his kiss sent a thrill tingling
along every nerve, and as her lips, soft and responsive,
parted under his, she knew denial was useless. Her arms
crept round his neck and as she relaxed against him, she
felt his body tense and harden. Without moving away he
half-turned, lifting her easily, and locked in each other's
arms, they sank down on the bed.

Melanie abandoned herself to the powerful emotions
surging through her. Too much had happened, too much
danger, too many narrow escapes. The last protective
layers had been peeled off with her wetsuit and there was
nowhere left for her to hide. Her fingers curled in his hair
and caressed his neck. He eased the robe aside and she
felt cool air on her hot skin. He stroked her back with
gentle fingers, leaving a wake of tiny flames. Palm on her
hip, he pushed her on to her back and, tearing his mouth
from hers, pressed his lips to her throat, the hollow of her
shoulder and her breast, teasing its rosy peak with his
tongue. She shuddered with delight and caught her
breath.

He raised his head and there was a kind of agony in his
face as he whispered her name. Then he possessed her
mouth once more. His body moved over hers and his
weight forced her down. In a split second her excitement,
the blossoming desire, were snuffed out like a candle-
flame in an icy blast of fear, as her brain shrieked its
silent warning. She had no chance to fight, to rationalise,
or beat it back, so swift and violent was its attack.

'No, no!' she gasped and, rigid, pushed him frantically
away, squirming from under him.

Luke sat back, eyes shocked, breathing harsh.
'Melanie? What's wrong?'

'I can't, I can't!' Her voice was thin and high.

He was struggling for control, his voice thick. 'Mel, for God's sake, we can't stop now!'

'Please,' she pushed with all her strength, her eyes huge, her face contorted, 'I can't.'

Luke rolled away and sat on the edge of the bed, resting his elbows on his knees as he raked both hands through his hair. 'I don't understand. You wanted me, Melanie, as much as I wanted you. You can't deny that.'

Her chest heaved as she dragged in lungfuls of air, clutching the robe around her. 'I'm not denying it.'

'What is it, then? Was I rushing you? What I feel for you, it's strong, Melanie, too strong sometimes. I've never felt for any woman what—when I think of what might have happened down in the wreck—if I'd lost you——' He broke off, shaking his head helplessly. He looked over his shoulder into her eyes. 'Do you know what I'm trying to say?'

She bit her lip and nodded.

'Do I have to spell it out? Is that what you're waiting for?'

She couldn't hide the quick hurt. 'No,' she said quietly, and sat up, hugging the robe around her, suddenly cold again, 'I've never bartered my feelings, Luke, for words or anything else.'

He swore under his breath and stood up, tightening the towel around his waist. His muscular back gleamed with perspiration. Needing an outlet for his perplexity and frustration, he began to pace the cabin. 'Isn't it the same for you?' he demanded hoarsely. 'Don't you feel—have I been kidding myself I was beginning to mean something to you?'

She smiled slowly, her eyes wet with tears. 'I love you, Luke.'

He stopped in mid-stride, confusion vivid on his face. 'You do?'

She nodded and wiped her eyes on her sleeve then hugged her knees.

'So—why, Mel?' he beseeched.

'This——' She swallowed. 'It's not your fault, believe me. It has nothing to do with you.'

He raked his hair again, then swung round. 'Paul. It's Paul, isn't it?'

She nodded briefly.

'Still in love with him, are you?' His voice was harsh.

Melanie's eyes widened as she stared up at him, seeing lines of pain and bitterness etched deeply on either side of his mouth. His features were taut and a muscle jumped spasmodically in his cheek as he waited tensely for her reply. 'No, no, you've got it all wrong. I was never in love with Paul.'

He spread his hands. 'Then how can he keep coming between us like this? What the hell *do* you feel for him?'

'Hatred,' she said softly.

Luke was startled. 'Why, for God's sake? If you didn't love him, how can he be important enough to hate?' He sat on the edge of the bed and put a hand over hers. 'OK, so he was a swine to work with, but he's dead, part of the past. Forget him, Mel.'

'Do you think I don't want to?' she cried in anguish. 'I'd give ten years of my life to wipe him out of my thoughts, to stop having those nightmares. Do you have any idea what it's like to feel ashamed of something I couldn't prevent? To feel defiled—spoiled——' Her face crumpled and tears flooded her cheeks. 'He raped me,' the brutal words were torn from her, 'the night before he died—the fight——' She choked on a sob and hammered her knee with a clenched fist.

Luke stared at her, his face setting like stone. He seized her shoulders, forcing her to look at him. 'Why in God's name didn't you tell me? Why didn't you trust me?'

'Trust?' Her eyes were wild. 'I've known you a week, and since the moment we met my world has been upside down. I've thought and felt things I didn't know existed. I wasn't prepared—didn't expect—why should I have trusted you? I'd known Paul for years, called him friend and trusted him——' Her voice broke and her head fell forward on to her knees as her body convulsed with deep, racking sobs.

'Oh, Melanie!' Luke put his arms around her and drew her towards him. She stiffened momentarily, then, mentally and emotionally exhausted, sagged against his chest.

'No wonder you were so frightened!' He stroked her hair. 'Why the hell didn't Derek tell me? Warn me off?'

Melanie shook her head. 'He doesn't know. No one does, except you.'

His hand was still. 'No one? Why not?'

She swallowed hard. 'I—I couldn't, I was too ashamed.'

Luke tilted her chin and through her scalding tears she saw her own agony reflected in his eyes. 'Ashamed? Why, for God's sake? Because you weren't strong enough to fight off a man in peak physical condition who was behaving like a crazy animal? *You* were ashamed?' He drew a ragged breath, and held her closer. 'But why didn't you tell someone? The police, or a girl friend?'

She shrugged helplessly. 'I was too shocked and sick. I think I went a bit out of my mind. I couldn't believe—I thought he was my friend——'

She could not go on. Luke pressed his lips against her hair, her temple. 'The next morning Paul died. How could I tell anyone then? What good would it have done?'

His voice was hoarse. 'If he weren't dead I think I'd kill him myself for the pain he's caused you, the legacy of fear. If only you'd told me, Mel, I'd never have——'

'Wanted me?' The words slipped out. But she had to

know. Now he knew the truth would it change
everything? Her self-esteem had been shattered and on
bad days she felt defiled and degraded. How would *he*
regard her now? It took all the will-power she possessed
to raise her wet face and look directly into his eyes. He
held her gaze for a long moment, then said softly, 'I've
wanted you almost from the moment we met, but it's
grown into much more than that. That's the usual order
of things for a man, and I make no excuses or apologies
for it.' He drew his thumbs gently across her flushed
cheeks, wiping away the tears. 'Nothing I've learned in
the past few minutes changes the way I feel about you.'
The compassion in his voice was balm to her soul. There
had been no doubt, no hint of accusation.

She searched his face. 'Can you understand?'

'Why you didn't tell me?' He nodded, then smiled
wryly. 'But things would have been a lot easier if you had.
For a start I would——'

There was a hammering on the day cabin door and
Callum's voice called, 'Luke, will ye tak yon chest now?
Young Driscoll has a mind to open it and start with his
pictures. He's comin' tae see ye 'issel'.'

'Hang on a minute, Callum,' Luke shouted. He stood
up and leaning over, cupped Melanie's face. 'Will you be
all right?'

'Of course,' she gulped, and rummaged in her pocket
for a tissue. 'You'd better go.' She managed a watery
smile. 'You'll get no peace until he's seen it. After all, if
he hadn't been injured, he'd have been with us.'

Luke gave her a quick kiss on the cheek. 'We'll talk
later.' He went out of her cabin, calling, 'Come in,
Callum.'

'Is the lassie a'right?' Melanie heard the engineer ask.

'A bit shaken, but she'll be fine,' Luke replied as he
closed the door. The voices rumbled on, but Melanie
didn't listen. She scrambled off the bed and looked at

herself in the mirror above the wash-basin. Her eyes were red, and felt hot and gritty, and her nose shone. She grimaced, filled the basin with cold water and plunged her face in several times. Drying it, she felt refreshed and much calmer. Luke was right: the awful secret had been a festering sore inside her. But telling him had released the poison and the pressure, and now she really could begin to look forward instead of remaining locked in the past. He had been so kind, so incredibly understanding.

She dressed in the blue cotton trousers and shirt Herbie had washed and ironed for her, combed her hair and left it loose to dry.

There was more hammering on the outside door and she heard her brother's voice, sharp with excitement, followed by Luke's deeper, quieter tones. After a quick glance in the mirror to ensure all traces of tears had been erased, she went out into the day cabin.

Callum had gone and Luke had managed to pull on a fresh pair of faded jeans and a clean black T-shirt. The chest, resting on some old towels, sat on his desk. '—each item photographed for the record,' he was saying, 'but an inventory will have to be made first, so you'd better leave it until after lunch.'

'OK,' Derek agreed. 'I'll swap the lenses and get everything ready. Hi, Mel.' He smiled at her over Luke's shoulder. 'You won't be invited back if you keep leaving expensive equipment all over the seabed!'

It took her a few seconds to adjust, so different was this from the last time they had spoken. Then she realised, from the anxiety in his eyes, and the effort it was costing him to hold the grin in place, that he was desperately trying to make amends. Apologising was not Derek's forte; he had always been a fervent believer in 'least said, soonest mended.'

Knowing only too well how stress could provoke words instantly regretted, Melanie smiled at her brother.

'Unless you can find wrecks that stay put, I don't think I want to play this game again anyway. Besides, I've grown quite fond of breathing regularly, and being rationed doesn't really appeal.'

Derek's smile faded. 'Callum said it was a pretty close thing.'

Melanie shrugged. 'At least we didn't have the sharks waiting for an early lunch.'

'Speaking of which,' Luke looked at his watch, 'I shall have a sandwich on the bridge. I want to return to Fort Dauphin as soon as possible and get this little lot,' he patted the chest, 'the hell off my boat. Derek, you'd better get back to your cabin.'

'Oh yes, sure,' he said quickly. 'Er—Luke, can I bring Selena to the saloon for dinner this evening? I mean, it will be celebration time and I don't want to be stuck in the cabin while everyone else hears how you got the chest out. She won't be in the way, I promise, and after all, she can't tell anyone while we're all together.'

After a brief pause, Luke nodded. 'OK, make it six-thirty. Now the diving is finished we can come off the wagon.' He grinned at Melanie. 'François has been hoarding some bottles of Dom Perignon from our last job. I think tonight might be a good time to open them.'

'Oh boy!' Derek rubbed his hands together, 'This is going to be some party!' He went back to his cabin, chuckling.

Herbie appeared in the doorway. 'About lunch, Captain?'

'Sandwiches and coffee on the bridge in half an hour for me. Melanie?'

'I'd better have a tray in here. I must get the log up to date.'

'And next door, sir. Mr Driscoll and his—er—guest?'

'Trays for them both,' Luke was firm.

'Of course, sir.' The steward didn't quite click his heels

together, and departed as smoothly as he had come.

'Right, one more thing.' Luke opened a drawer in his desk and took out a heavy screwdriver. As he jammed the chisel-like edge under the lid of the chest, Melanie winced.

Luke glanced at her. 'Do you fancy going back down for the key?'

'Not much,' she smiled. 'In any case, that lock looks as if it's solid with corrosion. It's just—' she shrugged, '—I don't know, I suppose I'm just being silly.'

'Didn't you ever break into your piggy bank when you were little?'

'Yes, but that was different.'

'Melanie, we risked our lives for this. Don't you think it would be a good idea to make sure it's what we came for?'

'Of course. Go on.'

As he inserted the flat blade, Melanie held her breath. After several seconds' steadily increased pressure which made the muscles in Luke's arm and shoulder stand out like bunched rope, the lock gave with an agonised squeal, and the lid flew back.

Melanie gasped.

'Well, just look at that!' Luke breathed. They stood side by side gazing down at the rainbow-hued tangle of gold and jewels that gleamed and sparkled in the light of the desk lamp.

Luke picked up one end of a necklace which, when he lifted it out, turned out to be a collar of gold filigree studded with emeralds. There were bracelets of gold twisted like rope, with clasps shaped into snakes' heads and sapphires for eyes. There were anklets and toe-rings; pearls shaped like teardrops with a glowing pink lustre; hair ornaments of gold so finely crafted they looked like lace, hung with garnets; and a magnificent waterfall necklace of rubies.

Melanie's eyes were like saucers. 'I—I've never seen anything like this,' she murmured, picking up a beautiful pigeon's blood ruby solitaire, then placing it reverently on the growing pile beside the now half-empty chest.

Luke checked his watch again. 'I'd better get to the bridge. Will you make a list of this lot?' he gestured to the pile of jewels.

'Me?' Melanie was startled.

'Someone has to,' he said reasonably, 'and you said you'd be doing the log anyway. When you've finished, Derek can photograph it all.'

'What for? I mean, why is it necessary?'

'Call it a sort of insurance.' He kissed the back of her neck. 'Have fun,' he grinned. 'I'll see you later.'

'But, Luke,' she called, uncertainly, 'you can't just leave me here with all this!'

'Why not?' His eyes gleamed with amusement. 'I trust you.' He went out, closing the door softly.

Melanie stared down at the heap. She couldn't begin to imagine its worth. She cradled a velvety black pearl in her palm, marvelling at its weight. Then, unable to resist the temptation, she picked up the ruby necklace and fixing it around her neck, hurried into her cabin. Tucking the neck of her shirt out of the way, she twisted her hair up, holding it with one hand, and gazed at her reflection, awed by the rich, glowing beauty of the stones.

The outer door opened and the steward came in with her lunch.

'What do you think, Herbie, is it me?' Melanie came out of her cabin and struck a pose.

Placing the tray on the chart table, the steward eyed her throat critically. 'Very nice, miss,' he allowed. 'But with your colouring, I think emeralds would be a better choice.' He glimpsed the wetsuit still lying on the floor. 'I'll remove that, miss.'

Melanie unhooked the necklace and laid it back on the

pile as the steward came past her with the suit folded over his arm. 'Herbie, how can you be so—so calm about all this?'

He smiled. 'I've been with the Captain a long time, miss. There isn't much surprises me any more. I daresay you'll find out for yourself. Enjoy your lunch, miss.' Before she could ask him what he meant, he'd gone.

After the quickest lunch she'd ever eaten, Melanie spread a clean towel across the chart table and carefully laid out each piece of jewellery.

Even the dazzling beauty of the gems could not push Luke entirely from her thoughts. She realised now just how afraid she had been that on learning the truth he would reject her. But he hadn't. Everything was going to be all right. She loved him so much. With difficulty she dragged her mind back to the job, writing a detailed description of each item, carefully checking the number and size of the stones. She was half-way through when Derek came in.

'Wow!' he breathed, his eyes widening.

'Hi, you'd better start at that end,' Melanie pointed, 'I haven't finished my notes on these.' She swivelled round in her chair. 'What about Selena? I thought——'

Derek dug in his jeans' pocket and held up a key. 'She's got plenty of books and magazines and I promised I wouldn't be long.' He pushed the key back in his pocket. 'Bloody inhuman way to treat anybody,' he muttered, and began adjusting the flash mechanism on his camera. 'Especially her. She's been through enough.'

'But what if——' Melanie stopped, then decided to risk the question. 'Derek, you have to admit, her—arrival was a bit odd. I mean, what if she is involved in something we don't know about?'

'Selena? That's ridiculous. That poor girl's had one hell of a life. If you only knew——' He broke off and raised the camera, focusing on the gold and emerald collar which lay at the top left-hand corner of the towel. 'Hell, you're not interested.'

'Yes, I am,' she said quietly.

He lowered the camera and swung round. 'Why? So you can tell me what a fool I'm being?'

'No,' she replied, 'so I can perhaps see what you see.'

He refocused the camera and the flash buzzed as it recharged. He took a second shot, then as he bent over the next piece, began to talk. It spilled out in an indignant tumble.

Selena was the illegitimate daughter of a young Irish domestic who had given in to her wealthy employer's advances and been sacked when his wife found out. Her mother moved from job to job, and most of Selena's babyhood had been spent with child-minders. Eventually her mother, weary of responsibility, and offered marriage provided no visible reminders of previous liaisons were included, left Selena with foster-parents who had been very kind to her. But they had been killed in a motorway pile-up from which she had escaped without injury. So at fifteen she had been placed with another set of foster-parents. But though still emotionally a child, she had developed physically, and the eldest son kept pestering her. When eventually she plucked up the courage to tell his mother, the woman accused her first of lying, then of deliberately provoking her son. She had run away, and tried to find her real mother.

'Did she find her?' asked Melanie.

Derek nodded. 'Only now she had four toddlers and a husband who drank. She told Selena to clear off.'

At sixteen, after meeting a photographer who had promised her modelling work if she didn't mind taking her bra off, Selena was earning enough to rent a tiny fourth-floor flat in an old tenement building. She furnished it from junk shops. The kitchen was a stone sink and an old stove behind a curtain. But she kept it scrupulously clean, and each time she had some cash to spare, bought herself another flowering pot-plant for the windowsill. It was her first real home, her refuge from the world, and she guarded it jealously.

The next five years saw her break into fashion work as the health and fitness craze ushered in a curvier shape. Then, after meeting a producer at a party, she was offered a part in a film. Her two lines as an aerobics instructor ended up on the cutting room floor, but someone must have talked about her, for a month later along came the chance of a lifetime.

'Or so it seemed to her,' Derek said. 'According to the two gorillas it was to be a film of great social significance set on a beautiful island in the Indian Ocean.' His voice was full of bitter mockery. 'Five hundred a week, all expenses and a generous bonus if they could bring it in within a month.'

'It must have been tempting,' Melanie admitted, 'but what about the script? Surely she would have seen——'

'They had an answer for everything. The scripts weren't available because the director had ordered rewrites, but would be ready when she arrived. The rest of the cast had gone on ahead with the crew to do some preliminary shots. She was the last to be chosen because they'd been searching for someone with just her qualities. They had too.'

'What do you mean?'

'They'd done their homework. Apart from Selena's face and figure, which speak for themselves, she's alone in the world. No parents, no one to worry about her, to ask awkward questions, persuade her against it. And once they got their hooks in, they didn't let up. They piled on the pressure about it being a stepping stone to stardom, tossed well-known directors' names about like confetti, hinted that a refusal might damage her chances of future offers, and that she'd have to decide quickly as time was money and there were other girls queueing up to take advantage of this fantastic opportunity. Well, she'd had a lean couple of months. One sportswear company she modelled for had gone bust, another had cancelled its catalogue due to falling sales. So despite some niggling doubts, she decided to go and make the most of the break. She had to sign a sheaf of forms, travel warrants, insurances, vaccination and Customs declarations. She couldn't remember them all.'

'And the contract was slipped in amongst them?' Melanie tapped her chin with her pen.

Derek nodded. 'She's sure it happened like that, and I believe her.' He shot a sideways glance at his sister, defying doubt.

Melanie recalled Selena's heavy make-up, clinging low-cut dress and mane of chestnut hair. Derek caught her rueful smile.

'What's so funny?' But he sounded more curious than angry.

She leaned back, surveying her slim figure. 'I certainly didn't look like that at twenty-one.'

He laughed. 'Guess you're more the greyhound type, kid. Still, why should you care, you've got the whole crew eating out of your hand, and Luke Avery isn't exactly hiding his interest.'

Melanie's face grew warm, but she said nothing.

Derek stood back from the table. 'That's the lot. I suppose I'd better get a shot or two of the casket as well.' When he finished he eyed it thoughtfully. 'That's changed quite a few lives one way and another.' He patted Melanie on the shoulder. 'I guess we both found a lot more than we bargained for on this trip.'

Her smile was quick and reply fervent. 'You can say that again!'

'See you at dinner. And, Mel—thanks.'

'What for?' She looked surprised.

He shrugged. 'Whatever.'

She turned back to the table and began replacing the jewels. There was still the log to do.

At six-forty she was showered and dressed. On impulse she had put on a cotton skirt and matching sleeveless top prettily patterned in tan and apricot with touches of green and white. After brushing her hair till it shone she had drawn it back off her face in two combs and was putting the finishing touches to her light make-up when she heard Luke enter the day cabin. Glancing out of the porthole, she could see they were once more alongside the jetty. The afternoon's work had so engrossed her, she had been quite unaware of the engines or the boat's movement.

What now? she wondered. What happens next? She tried to think forward, to conjure some vision of the future, but her mind remained blank. She felt a tremor of apprehension, of uncertainty, and sat down on the bed to put on her sandals. She could hear Luke humming as he changed and banished the momentary doubt. Tonight was a celebration. The mission was almost complete. Despite all the problems they had achieved what they'd set out to do. As for Luke and herself, they would talk later, he had promised.

He tapped briefly on the connecting door and without waiting for her reply walked in.

'I don't know why you bother to knock,' she remarked with mild exasperation.

Showered and shaved, his thick hair neatly combed and already escaping into unruly waves, he was wearing the beige safari suit. 'Nor do I,' he said blandly. 'I won't bother in future.' He held out his hands.

'That wasn't what I meant.' She went to him, smiling.

'I know.' His mouth was cool and tasted of mint toothpaste. But as the kiss lengthened, growing deeper, more intimate as his arms tightened around her, her head began to swim. She sensed he was holding back, trying to control the powerful feelings that threatened to engulf them both. At last they broke apart and he held her away from him, his eyes clouded with desire. 'I don't think I can take much more of this,' he muttered.

Her breasts rose and fell with her rapid breathing and she glowed from the heat he had kindled in her body.

'We have to talk,' he said abruptly, moving away from her. 'There are things I haven't told you. I didn't expect—look, there's no time now, but after the party ...' He left the sentence unfinished and touched her cheek lightly, searching her eyes, but for what she didn't know. Once more apprehension rippled through her like a cold breath. A smile lifted the corners of his mouth as, with an abrupt change of mood, he offered her his arm. 'Let's go and celebrate. I reckon we've earned it!'

Closing her mind to everything but the moment, Melanie slipped her arm through his and smiled up at him. 'I'll drink to that.'

Callum and Billo had obviously dressed for the occasion. Billo's crisp white shirt was set off by a neatly knotted blue and red tie, while Callum was resplendent in the gaudiest Hawaiian shirt Melanie had ever seen. It was predominantly scarlet and lime-green, and topped by the engineer's ginger hair and beard, the effect was startling. Herbie had discarded his white jacket in favour of an Aertex shirt. François and Alain had removed their aprons, and François wore a navy short-sleeved shirt and crimson neckerchief over baggy grey flannels. It was the first time Melanie had seen him without a Gauloise adhering to his lower lip. Alain had chosen black canvas drainpipe jeans and a pink, purple and lilac striped collarless shirt. Derek was in his blue safari suit, but it was Selena who drew Melanie's eye as she and Luke walked into the room to a ragged cheer.

Wearing the green shirt knotted under her full bosom

and a pair of Derek's jeans, her chestnut hair tied back in a ponytail to reveal a face dusted with freckles and bare of make-up, this fresh-complexioned girl bore scant resemblance to the heavily made-up woman Melanie had seen in the hotel bar. Their eyes met, Melanie's mirroring her surprise, Selena's a hostility swiftly replaced by blankness beyond which it was impossible to see.

François brought in the champagne with a flourish, and though the bucket was orange polythene, it held plenty of ice, and the napkins folded around the bottles were snowy white and starched to perfection.

Luke popped the corks, glasses were filled and everyone stood for the toast. Luke raised his glass. Melanie expected something about the success of their mission, or a joke about the hazards that had dogged them and the narrow escape they had had, so his quiet words, 'They that go down to the sea in ships, that do business in great waters,' came as a surprise. Derek caught her eye and shrugged imperceptibly, but Melanie, recognising the lines as part of a Psalm, sensed that this salute was an important tradition for Luke and his crew. Tonight it honoured the memory of Captain Elliot and the crew of the *Buckingham*, and acknowledged their own good fortune in surviving the storm and all the other dangers. The toast was drunk in silence. But as the glasses were lowered, the mood changed and François bustled Alain back into the galley to bring in the first course.

The avocado mousse was followed by lobster. The champagne flowed and demands grew for details of the finding and recovery of the chest. Luke suggested Melanie tell it, but she shook her head, laughing. 'I can't remember much about it, I was too scared.'

So while they ate, Luke related the story, using condiments and cutlery to illustrate the broken furniture. At one point he caught her eye and with a brief movement of his head indicated the door. She slipped unnoticed from the table and went to fetch the chest.

Returning to the saloon, clasping her priceless burden, Melanie paused for a moment in the doorway. Everyone was talking. The atmosphere was a heady mixture of laughter, good food, fine wine and the comradeship that comes from shared experience. Derek's head was close to Selena's as he explained something. The pleasure on his face and animated gestures revealed an interest not solely sympathetic.

Melanie switched her gaze to Selena, who watched Derek as she listened. Her smile was fond and genuine, but her eyes were reserved. Which was hardly surprising, Melanie thought. Considering her life and the more recent events, who could blame her for being wary?

Luke caught sight of her and raised one dark brow, obviously wondering why she was hanging about. She went in at once, and with a mock fanfare placed the chest in the centre of the table.

There was a moment's absolute silence, then obeying Luke's gesture, she opened the lid. Five heads craned forward, five pairs of eyes widened and there was a collective intake of breath, then exclamations of varying strengths in both French and English. Even Luke, Herbie, Derek and Melanie, who had already seen the jewels, found themselves drawn once more to the shimmering display. The pieces were passed from hand to hand. Comments and laughter erupted at Callum's dour remarks. But, Melanie noticed, even he could not entirely disguise his awe. Selena made no effort to touch the jewels at first, darting puzzled glances at Luke, but when it became obvious that by being at the table she was entitled to take part, she was drawn like everyone else to finger, examine and admire the magnificent gems.

An hour later Luke suggested it was time to call it a night. The chest was refilled. François and Herbie began to clear the table and Alain was sent to begin washing up. Billo said he'd lend Callum a hand checking a troublesome battery in the engine room. Selena said a shy goodnight to everyone, and Derek, his arm protectively around her shoulders, guided her out.

'Go on back to the cabin,' Luke said softly to Melanie, passing her the chest. 'There are one or two things I still have to take care of, but I shouldn't be more than an hour.' His gaze was warm and so full of promise, her heart turned over.

Once in the cabin, she put the chest in a safe place, then went through to her sleeping quarters and kicked off her sandals. It had been a wonderful evening. They were a marvellous bunch. How much she would have missed if Luke had not persuaded her to stay after their first disastrous meeting. So much had happened in such an incredibly short time. She had conquered one of her darkest fears and was determined to overcome the others; she had finally found the courage to open her heart to life and love.

She stretched, whirling round in the tiny cabin, and smiled. Maybe the champagne had something to do with it, but she felt light and floating and deliciously dreamy. 'Don't be long, Luke,' she whispered. There was so much she wanted to know. And what of the future? She still had several more weeks' holiday, but what were his plans now the chest had been recovered? What was to happen to the jewels?

Suddenly the little cabin seemed too small and she had an overpowering need for space and fresh air. Closing the door quietly, she padded on bare feet along the passage and up to the deck.

The sea slapped against the jetty and several yards beyond broke in a welter of white foam on the sand. The palms whispered and sighed as she lifted her head to gaze at the limitless sky seeded with countless diamond-bright stars. The gentle, sweet-scented breeze cooled and caressed her skin as she strolled slowly towards the bow. The island seemed to be reaching out, weaving its magic around her. It was not the alien place she had first thought. That had been a reflection of her own fear and vulnerability. But everything was different now. She inhaled deeply, filling her lungs with the fragrance of jasmine and cloves. A smile of gratitude and contentment curved her mouth and turning in the shadow of the bridge she decided to return to the cabin and wait for Luke.

'Where does he think you are at this moment?'

The sound of his voice made her jump. She looked round but couldn't see him, then realised one of the windows on the bridge was open. She didn't hear the person he was speaking to reply. Then his voice came again.

'I promise you it will be all right, no one need ever know.'

In the shadows, her hand half-way to the door handle, Melanie found herself unable to move. Who *was* he talking to?

'I've handled situations like this before.' She heard the confidence in his deep voice. 'The main thing is to make damned sure neither of them realise they've been lied to. Can you manage that?'

Frozen by a premonition of impending disaster, Melanie held her breath, and her world, so bright and new and full of promise, crumbled to dust as Selena's throaty laugh floated out into the night.

'I'll give the performance of my life!'

CHAPTER TEN

FEELING she might shatter into a million fragments, Melanie crept back to the cabin. There had to be an explanation—after all, she had heard only part of the conversation. Her nails bit into her palms as she clung desperately to reason. Luke would explain. When he returned to the cabin he would tell her why Selena had sneaked away to this secret meeting.

The doubts and apprehension that had plagued her before dinner returned in full force. What if he didn't? How could she ask without revealing that she had listened? Even if he did not assume she had been spying on him, he might still choose not to tell her the truth. After all, hadn't he said the main thing was to make sure—no, to make *damned* sure neither of them realised they had been lied to? That could only mean Derek and herself. She felt sick. Not once during dinner had he given the slightest indication that he had even spoken to Selena since Derek brought her on board. But then he was a practised liar, wasn't he? He had said as much. 'I've handled these situations before.' To whom was he referring, Selena or herself?

She had only known him a week. For her it had been the most momentous week in her life, but for him? Had she been just a 'situation'? One of dozens he had 'handled'? Was Selena about to replace her?

No, she couldn't believe that of Luke. He had been kind and gentle with her. Yet he had not been talking to Selena as to a stranger, but rather as if he knew her, or was at least expecting her.

Had his anger at her appearance on board been just a

170

pretence, another lie?

No, no, it couldn't be. For if that were true surely it would mean that his behaviour towards herself was also a lie. The kisses which had stirred her so deeply, drawing her out of the black pit of horror into which Paul's drunken assault had plunged her, and marked the transition of respect and liking into love, they would have meant nothing more to Luke than convenient physical pleasure.

She closed her eyes. She could not accept that, she wouldn't believe it. Yes, he wanted her, he had admitted it, but he had also said that wanting had grown into something more. Yet hadn't he warned her there were things he had *not* told her, because he had not expected— what? Selena to turn up just then? Or Melanie to fall in love with him? Had that not been part of the plan, not budgeted for in the demands of the operation?

Had she been merely a distraction, useful to help pass non-working hours, but a problem now that the mission was almost over, so much sooner than they had expected?

He had needed her professional assistance during preparation and diving. She had done her job, and done it well, but it was over now. So, thanks very much and goodbye? Oh no, no, *no!*

Galvanised into action, Melanie dragged out her case and in feverish haste hauled open the wardrobe and drawers and began flinging her clothes into it. She couldn't stay here. She had to get away. She needed time to think, and that would be impossible with Luke due back at any moment. One look would tell him something had happened, and she wasn't ready for his questions yet. She didn't even want to see him; it would only confuse her even more. She loved him, yet in her imagination could picture him, tall and ruggedly handsome, standing before her, quite relaxed, one dark brow raised in surprise, his blue eyes alight with mockery and amuse-ment. Of course it wasn't meant to be permanent, just natural reaction to the pressures and danger. You surely didn't take it *seriously?*

Melanie shut the case and pressed her fists to her temples. 'No, no, *no!*' she whispered, fighting down hysteria. She heard a door slam and jumped as though electrified. But it was not Luke, for through the bulkhead she heard Selena's voice, then her brother's raised in exclamation, followed by laughter. At the warm, happy sound, Melanie's eyes filled with scalded tears. How could she tell him? What would she say? Nothing, especially tonight. He wouldn't believe her. He would have to find out for himself. There was no other way he would accept it.

Dashing the tears away, she quickly locked the case and grabbed her handbag then hesitated. Should she leave a note? But what could she possibly say, 'Gone to think things over, love Melanie'? At least with all her clothes gone, no one would imagine she had fallen overboard.

She hurried through the day cabin, her eyes fixed firmly on the door. She didn't want to look at anything that would remind her of Luke, of what they had shared during this intense, demanding, claustrophobic week. She opened the door and peered up and down the passage. Her heart was beating so fast and so loudly she felt light-headed. Ice-cold perspiration dewed her body and her grip on the case was slipping.

She flew along the passage, up the stairs and on to the deck, the case bumping against her legs, and making her arm muscles scream in protest. She glanced about her in the starlit darkness, her overwrought senses hearing the baying of hounds at her heels. Nothing moved and there was no sound but that of wind and sea.

Darting from the hatch, her sandalled feet making a

soft, slapping sound, she looked over the side. The tide was on the rise and the deck was a couple of feet below the level of the jetty. Looking round, with every nerve screaming at her to hurry, yet terrified of making any noise which might bring someone to investigate, Melanie hefted her case over the rail and on to the jetty. She laid her bag on top, and with one last glance over her shoulder, scrambled up on to the stone and concrete quay, grazing both knees in her haste.

Panting from exertion and nervous strain, she grabbed her bags and walked as fast as she could off the quay and along the road towards the hotel. She did not look back.

She paused on the step, dragging in lungfuls of air, trying desperately to collect herself, to look as if her arrival so late in the evening was nothing out of the ordinary.

Though the door was unlocked, the foyer was deserted, as were the bar and lounge. Leaving her case beside the desk, Melanie went searching for someone to give her a key. She eventually found the manager in the kitchen, making himself a pot of coffee. She had obviously startled him, but as she stumbled through her rehearsed story about a radio message requiring her urgently in the capital, and wanting to arrange transport as early as possible in the morning, his face cleared. 'Naturally, I expect to pay for any inconvenience to you and your staff,' she added, and breathed a sigh of relief as his face lit up at the mention of money.

'That is most generous, Miss Driscoll,' he said smoothly. 'As it happens, I myself have to go to Fianarantsoa early tomorrow morning, and I would be delighted to give you a lift. It will get you part of the way to the capital.'

Melanie was shaken. She hadn't expected that. Her hasty plan had been intended only to get her into the hotel, to give her a breathing space. Her mind raced, but she was too weary and confused to come up with an excuse not to take up his offer. She'd try and work something out later; all she wanted now was to be alone. 'Thank you, that is most kind.'

They returned to the desk and he handed her a key, then reached for the register.

'I've put you to enough trouble already,' she said quickly, dredging up her sweetest smile. 'Could we leave that until the morning? I'll sign it the moment I come down.' As she spoke she was moving towards the stairs and her stifled yawn was not a pretence. 'I really am awfully tired—please excuse me.'

He shrugged and nodded and left the book where it was. She wanted to ask him not to say she was here if anyone required, but to do so might arouse his suspicions. At least she had avoided signing in.

As she climbed the stairs she looked at the key tag and realised it was the same room she had stayed in on the night of her arrival, before she had seen her brother, or knew of Luke Avery's existence.

She let herself in, locked the door behind her and switched on the bedside light. The familiarity of the room was a slight shock. It was exactly the same as it had been a week ago, and its sameness was a vivid contrast to the changes in her.

Totally drained, but too tense to sleep, she opened her case. Taking out the terrycloth robe, she undressed quickly and put the robe on, wrapping it tightly around her, grateful for the warmth of its thick, soft folds. Rolling up the skirt and blouse, she tossed them into the case and took out the trousers and shirt she would wear the following morning. Mechanically she washed her face, bathed the blood from her knees, then cleaned her teeth and brushed her hair. Then she closed the case, tossed her bag down beside it, and turning off the light, lay on the bed and stared at the ceiling.

It was almost midnight. With the jewels now on board the boat, secrecy was even more important, so it was unlikely Luke would wish to draw attention to himself by storming the hotel in the middle of the night to look for her. And it was, she realised, the most obvious place to look. There was nowhere else she could have gone. Assuming, of course, that he *wanted* to find her.

It was possible he would see her flight as a blessing. It would save any scenes. He would not have to make explanations, answer questions, think up lies. Of course, he might find it a little awkward explaining her sudden disappearance to Derek, but no doubt he'd find a plausible reason which Derek, because he was unaware of the scope of her relationship with Luke, and still totally absorbed in Selena, would accept.

She turned on her side, drawing her legs up, hugging herself as the numbness started to wear off. As she vainly fought each lacerating doubt, agonised despair began to overwhelm her. Not Luke. She couldn't have been so wrong, not again, not so soon. Was it her? Had she lost all sense of judgment? Was she utterly gullible? Totally naïve? A gift to any slick con-man who could spin a half-convincing yarn?

In a desperate effort to escape the clamour in her head, she jumped off the bed and went to the window, pulling back the curtains to look down on to the garden, and beyond to the beach and creaming surf. To the far right she could see the boat tied to the jetty. Light spilled from the portholes, but the bridge was now in darkness. Shifting her gaze abruptly, she missed the figure running silently from the direction of the hotel along the quay to climb carefully on to the boat.

She stared at the dark water, but saw only Luke as he had been that first day, walking calmly past her into this very room, announcing that he wasn't used to discussing business in hotel corridors, telling her she had no logical reason for turning him down, using her own arguments against her before she could even voice them.

Now she had allowed herself one memory, she could not shut off the flood, and leaned against the window, powerless to escape the images bombarding her. Luke grilling her about the medical, refusing to let her dive; showing her the lemurs as they walked in the forest; lying on the river bank watching her paddle; dark and supple in his wetsuit. She heard the roughness in his voice as he insisted she trust him; saw his eyes, warm with gentle amusement at her shyness as they lay together on the sand and he smoothed oil into her back, and clouded with passion as they broke from an embrace.

She felt a stirring deep inside. 'No!' she moaned, burying her face in her hands, and whirled away from the window to fall across the bed. Her weeping was silent. Her body shook and the cover grew damp beneath her face, but the pain remained. Eventually, utterly exhausted, she slept.

Dawn was breaking when she woke, stiff and hot-eyed, glad to escape the restless dreams. She had slept where she had fallen, on top of the covers, still wearing her robe. For a moment she didn't know where she was, but that respite lasted only a split second, then memory returned and with it the dull, hopeless ache of desolation.

She dressed and was bathing her swollen eyes with cold water when there was a gentle knock on the door. Her heart thumped so hard she felt sick. Could it be? Had he come? She clutched the towel, paralysed by uncertainty. How she longed to see him, but would he lie?

Another gentle tap, then the manager's voice called softly, 'Miss Driscoll, I have some coffee for you.'

Warily, Melanie dropped the towel and unlocked the door. The manager was alone. He handed her a cup and saucer.

'Perhaps, to save time, you—er——' he cleared his throat delicately, 'might wish to settle your account now?'

'Oh, yes of course.' She put the coffee on the dressing table and fumbled for her purse. She handed him several notes, realising as his face lit up and the money vanished into his pocket that she had given him far too much, but she was beyond caring.

'So glad to have been of assistance,' he murmured smoothly. 'We shall leave in ten minutes. I'll take your case, shall I?'

Melanie nodded, laid her robe and toilet bag on top of her crumpled clothes, then closed the lid and locked it.

The manager picked up the case. 'You'll find the car at the back of the hotel. It's a brown Range Rover.' He closed the door and she heard his footsteps receding.

Her hand trembled as she lifted the cup. She told herself it was the scalding coffee that brought tears to her eyes. She had been with Luke in that same car when they had almost collided with the funeral procession and he had told her of the beliefs and customs of the Malagasy people, and revealed the true purpose of his visit to the island.

'*Vazaha*,' she whispered, replacing the cup with shaking fingers, 'heart thief.'

Wiping her eyes, she collected her comb from the dressing table and put on her sandals. On impulse she went to the window. He hadn't come. He had to have known she was not on board. He had to have known the hotel was the only place she could be. But he had not come. There was nothing to keep her here, no reason to hope any longer.

The rising sun turned the water to liquid gold, and a muted rumble drew Melanie's attention to the jetty. At first she didn't believe it. She closed her eyes tight, then looked once more. There was no mistake. Billo's stocky figure unhooked the stern mooring rope and jumped back on board. The gap between the bow and the jetty was already widening, and with the stern line released, the boat moved in a smooth arc and headed towards the open sea.

Melanie put her hand over her mouth. Luke was leaving. No message, no attempt to see her or explain. He was simply turning his back on her and going away.

She should have known, should have realised. He was a proud man, used to command, to obedience. She had run. Whatever his personal feelings, he would not run after her. Now it was too late. Deep inside her something shrivelled and died.

With empty eyes she turned from the window, picked up her bag and walked out of the room, quietly closing the door on part of her life and the whole of her heart.

Reaching the top of the stairs, she looked down and saw the two men who had threatened Selena reading a note, one craning over the other's shoulder. They were unshaven and had obviously dressed in a hurry. The one holding the piece of paper swore violently in French, and the other waved at the door, talking very fast with much gesticulation. The first one nodded and stuffed the paper into his pocket and they both ran out of the hotel. They had not seen Melanie, and as she reached the bottom of the stairs, she looked through the window and saw them racing towards the jetty, too late to recapture the star of their film. As the distance between the boat's stern and the quay widened, so they had to be losing their chance of a fortune. In spite of everything Melanie was glad Selena had escaped their filthy clutches. One was waving his arms at the departing boat while the other ran up and down the quay, obviously looking for some seaworthy craft in which to give chase.

Melanie turned away. None of it concerned her any more. She supposed she would feel something later, but now she was quite numb. It was only possible to feel so much; after that, the mind simply short-circuited and went blank.

The manager was waiting in the car. Her case was on the back seat. She tossed her bag on top of it and climbed into the passenger seat, and they swung out on to the road.

He tried to draw her into conversation, but receiving no reply soon gave up. Vaguely, Melanie wondered at herself. It was not in her nature to be impolite, but she didn't owe him anything; the cash he had so readily pocketed was more than enough compensation for her silence.

She couldn't dismiss a niggling suspicion. It had been almost too much of a coincidence that he should be going north this morning. Was it possible that she had somehow been manipulated into leaving Fort Dauphin?

She closed her eyes and leaned her head back. That was ridiculous. It had been her decision. If he appeared keen to oblige it was only due to her over-generous payment. She couldn't blame anyone else. Her reaction to the whole business had been a total disaster.

They left the town and headed towards the mountains. Melanie kept her eyes shut, partly to discourage conversation, but mostly because she was too tired and too unhappy to care about the scenery.

A little while later she felt the vehicle turn left. Suddenly the road was no longer smooth. Her eyes flew open as they bumped and jolted over a rough track carved between the tall trees and tropical ferns of the rain forest.

'Where is this?' She leaned forward. 'Why have we left the main road?'

He did not look at her. 'It is necessary,' was all he said, then as they reached a fork in the path he pulled over and switched off the engine.

'Please wait here,' he said, and got out.

'Where are you going?' Melanie demanded sharply. The manager glanced round, gave an apologetic shrug and started running down the right-hand path. He disappeared into the forest and a few moments later she heard the roar of an engine and a battered truck rattled out on to the track and jolted away round the bend.

Melanie scrambled across the seat and leapt out on to the track. 'Hey!' she yelled, her voice cracking. 'Come back!' But the noise of the truck was fading and the dust had already settled on the rutted track.

A hand gripped her shoulder. She spun round and her hands flew to her mouth to stifle the scream.

'Come on,' Luke said grimly, 'we'd better get moving,' and bundled her back into the car, tossing an old kitbag on top of her case.

She sat, limp and unprotesting, as he swung the Range Rover back on to the track and followed the left fork up the incline.

'How—how did you get here?' she managed eventually.

'In the truck which is now on its way to Fianarantsoa.'

'No, I mean, what for? What are you doing——'

'Driving you to the capital,' he interrupted coldly. 'That's what you wanted, isn't it?'

She didn't answer for a long time. 'But how—I mean, I saw the boat leave.'

'Callum is taking it to Tamatave, I'm meeting him there.'

Her breath was beginning to function again. 'But you're not doing this just for me.' Though her tone was tentative, the words were a statement, not a question.

'You're right, I'm not.' She flinched. 'Part of the reason I'm here concerns the jewels, but why should you care?' He didn't look at her, yet beneath the cold dismissal she detected something that gave her the courage to press on.

'Call it professional interest,' she said quietly. 'I was involved in recovering them. I'd like to know how it ends.'

'But not enough to stay and find out,' he snarled at her, then looked out through the windscreen again, his expression bleaker than ever.

'I had—reasons.' She stared blindly ahead, compressing her lips to stop them trembling. She had her pride too. She would not beg for sympathy, nor would she give him the satisfaction of seeing her cry. She drew in a deep, shaky breath. 'Are you laying some sort of false trail?'

He shook his head. 'Not me, Derek and Selena.'

'What?' She looked at him quickly and as they reached the top of the hill, he wrenched the wheel around, pulled to a jerky stop and switched off the engine. They sat unmoving, the only sound the rattle of the keys as they swung in the ignition.

'If you'd just waited——' Luke began, but broke off, shaking his head abruptly. When he resumed speaking his voice was expressionless.

'You ran out on me last night, but you'll damn well listen now. When I was on the bridge last night, sending a radio message, Selena came to confess that there was more to her blackmail story than she'd told Derek. The two men do have their grubby fingers in the porn film racket, and the story Selena had told was absolutely true, as far as it went. Only that wasn't all of it. Those men were also fences, part of an international network dealing in stolen valuables, anything from paintings and silver to gems.'

'Pirates with business suits and briefcases,' Melanie murmured, recalling Luke's droll remark.

'They had had a tip-off about our operation. All Selena had to do for that contract to be torn up was to let them know as soon as we recovered the jewels.'

Melanie's thoughts were racing. Selena on the bridge, Luke sounding as though—'You knew, didn't you, about her?' she said softly.

'I'd been warned someone was on our trail, but I didn't know who. But when she turned up, it was a fair bet. I simply had to wait until she tried to pass a message or gave herself away. In the event she did neither. She came and told me the whole story. That was when we worked out a plan to double-cross the two men.'

Melanie reeled as if under a blow. But Luke simply went on talking, his eyes never leaving her face. 'She slipped ashore last night with a faked copy from my message pad, detailing the time of our proposed departure from Fort Dauphin, delayed because of engine trouble, and our arrival at the port of Tamatave, also the name of the man I was to meet, the arrangements for handing over the jewels, and where they would be taken. They swallowed it, hook, line and sinker. There was one nasty moment, when they tried to insist she stay with them to prove it wasn't a trick. But she managed to convince them that, having sought sanctuary on the boat, if she jumped ship while still in Fort Dauphin, we'd guess something was up and change all the arrangements. They let her go, and she listened at the keyhole long enough to hear them phone their contact in Tamatave to arrange for a helicopter to pick them up as soon as the boat left this evening's tide.'

'But it sailed at dawn——' Melanie began, the words trailing off as she recalled the two men's furious re-reading of the note and their frantic dash to the quay. She also recalled, with bell-like clarity, Luke's words 'We have to make damned sure neither of them realise they've been lied to.'

Her mouth was dry. It hadn't been Derek and herself he'd been referring to, but the two men. Which meant that the situations like this he had handled before had

had nothing to do with Selena as a woman, but as a plant, a spy.

'Who *are* you?' she asked in a barely audible whisper.

His blue eyes had never been so piercing. 'I intended to tell you last night. I started to, before we went to dinner, but there wasn't time, and afterwards——' He paused and shrugged, and Melanie flushed painfully under his merciless gaze.

She licked her papery lips. 'I thought——'

'You didn't wait to find out,' his tone was a whiplash, 'I assumed you overheard a fragment of conversation, but instead of waiting to talk it out with me, you packed and ran.' He turned his head away as if he found looking at her intolerable. 'So much for trust!' A muscle jumped in his jaw. He rested his elbow on the windowsill and raked a hand through his hair.

'You talk a lot about trust,' she said quietly, 'but you still haven't told me who you really are. Selena knows. She had to, that's why she agreed to the plan.'

'She didn't know when she came to the bridge. She came because of the kindness you and Derek had shown her.'

Melanie was startled. 'But I never saw her before dinner last night, and we barely spoke.'

'You gave her your clothes, brand new things you'd never worn. And Derek had listened and believed what she'd told him. He'd treated her with kindness and respect, and he hadn't tried to take advantage despite her past and sharing a cabin. Then when she ate with us, shared the champagne and heard the story of how we'd got the jewels out and was allowed to handle them like everyone else, she made up her mind to tell me the truth.'

Melanie regarded him with something akin to awe. 'You knew she would. You set it all up!'

'It was Derek's idea that she join us,' he pointed out.

'But you knew that by making her part of it, treating

her as one of us, you'd force her hand.'

'I hoped her conscience would win, I admit it.'

'But how did you know about the leak?'

'Before we started diving one of the Foreign Secretary's minions warned me by coded message that the
operation had been compromised, so I was——'

'Just a minute,' Melanie cut in, and sat bolt upright.
'Foreign Secretary——?' Her eyes widened as she
remembered Callum's initial reaction, 'Luke, are ye out
of your mind? She's no right for this.' Luke's insistence
on Derek taking photographs of every stage of the
operation and processing all the films on board, calling it
'a sort of insurance'. The secrecy, the pressure to get the
job finished as soon as possible, and the hints of
increasing risks. 'You work for the Government?'

He nodded.

'A sort of—*agent?*'

He half-smiled. 'Not exactly James Bond, I agree.'

She swallowed. 'And that was what you were going to
tell me?'

He nodded.

'Oh, my God!' She looked down at her hands, twisting
them in her lap, and shrugged helplessly. 'I thought——'
She couldn't go on. She had been totally wrong, but not in
the way she had imagined. She couldn't look at him. 'Oh,
Luke,' she whispered, 'I'm sorry.'

'Forget it,' he said flatly. 'Once I get the jewels into the
diplomatic bag and on their way to London, for me the
job is finished.'

Melanie's head flew up. 'What do you mean? I thought
they were on the boat.'

He shook his head. 'Double bluff,' he said succinctly,
and reaching over the back of the seat, picked up the
battered kitbag. He opened it, pulled out a rolled-up
towel and laying it on her lap, flipped it open.

Melanie gasped as the gems were revealed in all their

dazzling beauty.

'This is my last job,' he said quietly. 'I'm resigning.'

She looked at him. 'Is it my fault? Because you've—oh, what do they call it, blown your cover?' She was stricken. 'Luke, I'm sorry, I didn't——'

'Hush!' He leaned forward, laying a finger over her mouth. 'It is because of you, but has nothing to do with blown covers.' His smile faded and he seemed to be searching for words. 'It was a casual arrangement, and when I had only myself to think about, the risks were acceptable, but not any more.' He picked up a square-cut emerald ring, moving it so that the sunlight bounced off it and it flashed green fire. 'My share for the recovery of this little lot will be over a hundred thousand. The boat is mine, I've a first-rate crew and there are plenty of openings in oceanographic research.' He hesitated. 'So how do you feel about it?'

Bewildered, Melanie stared at him. Was he offering her some sort of job? 'How do I feel about what?'

'Marrying me,' he said softly, and lifting her left hand, he slid the ring on to her third finger. 'Only temporary, I'm afraid,' he grinned, 'but you can have another just like it.'

Melanie gazed at the ring, her eyes widening. Her other hand went to her mouth as her breath caught in her throat on a soft, almost silent, sob. She raised her head to look at Luke, joy lighting her features like a tropical dawn as slow tears welled in her eyes and spilled over to trickle down her cheeks. She could hardly believe it. After all that had happened, after she had lost her nerve and run out on him, after guessing what accusations she must have been harbouring, he still wanted to marry her.

'For God's sake say something,' he pleaded hoarsely.

She raised her eyes, her tear-stained face pale but radiant. 'Even if I'd never seen you again,' she whispered, 'I would have gone on loving you until the day

I died.'

A spasm crossed his face and his hand closed over her fingers. 'Then say you'll marry me. Life's not worth a candle without you—I learned that last night when I got back to the cabin and you'd gone.'

She searched his face. Her tongue snaked out to moisten her lips and she tried to speak, but the words she wanted wouldn't come. She closed her eyes briefly, biting the inside of her lip, then looked at him again with pleading in her gaze, and saw understanding dawn and relief spread over his features.

He slid his arm around her shoulders and drew her towards him, and lifting her left hand to his lips, kissed it tenderly. 'I love you, Melanie.' He released her hand and tilted her chin, looking deep into her eyes. 'We have a whole lifetime to wipe out memories of the past and the hurt you've suffered. I want to make love to you, and I want you to want me, but there's no rush, Mel. We have all the time in the world.' His arm tightened around and her and his fingers caressed her wet cheek as his mouth claimed hers.

Melanie's heart opened like a flower, releasing love and happiness beyond anything she had ever hoped for. Her arms crept around him and as she pressed closer, the towel slipped from her knees and the priceless jewels tumbled in a heap at her feet. Neither of them noticed.

A week later, as the sunset stained the waters of Table Bay a rich burgundy, and the lights of Capetown winked in the gathering dusk, Melanie stretched and opened her eyes.

In the dim light filtering through the curtained porthole she could just make out the froth of peach tulle tossed over the boxes she had not had time to unpack. The boat creaked and the fenders bumped gently against the wooden jetty of the marina.

She sighed in utter contentment. Callum and the others would be eating in the saloon. Derek and Selena had stayed ashore after the ceremony to go sightseeing.

Her thumb found the narrow gold band and rubbed it gently. It felt both strange and totally familiar. She turned on to her side and immediately Luke's warm, lean body curved around hers and his arm slipped under her own to cup her breast. She shivered deliciously and giggled as she felt him stir.

'My beautiful, desirable heart-thief,' he murmured in her ear, and she turned once more and with joy and pride welcomed him.

For the millions who can't read
Give the Gift of Literacy

One out of five adults in North America
cannot read or write well enough
to fill out a job application
or understand the directions on a bottle of medicine.

**You can change all this by joining the fight
against illiteracy.**

For more information write to:
Contact, Box 81826, Lincoln, Neb. 68501
In the United States, call toll free: 800-228-3225

**The only degree you need
is a degree of caring**

"This ad made possible with the cooperation of the Coalition for Literacy and the Ad Council."
Give the Gift of Literacy Campaign is a project of the book and periodical industry,
in partnership with Telephone Pioneers of America.

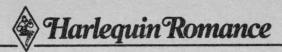
♦ Harlequin Romance

Coming Next Month

2845 WHEN LOVE FLIES BY Jeanne Allen
The strong sensitive man sitting beside a frightened American
admires her for facing her fear of flying. But Lindsey has a
greater fear—that of loving a man who, like her late father,
makes a living flying planes.

2846 TEMPERED BY FIRE Emma Goldrick
She's a young doctor, planning a quiet summer of
convalescence. He's an ex-military man, now writing a book
and planning a peaceful summer of work. They meet in New
England—and all plans for peace and quiet go up in flames!

2847 FUSION Rowan Kirby
Despite her successful career, a solicitor, whose husband
deserted her and their son, feels so emotionally insecure that
she struggles against getting involved again, even when she
finds a man she could love.

2848 IN LOVE WITH THE MAN Marjorie Lewty
Delighted to be part of a fact-finding team of Tokyo, a
computer operator's pleasure is spoiled when her big boss
unexpectedly accompanies them and thinks she's an
industrial spy.

2849 STAIRWAY TO DESTINY Miriam MacGregor
Delcie, a typist, tired of catering to the need of her
overprotective aunts, decides to work for a renowned
New Zealand author at his sheep station. There she learns
about her own needs . . . as a woman.

2850 BEYOND HER CONTROL Jessica Steele
Brooke rushes to France to rescue her young sister from a case
of puppy love for a worldly, wealthy chateau owner—only to
fall in love with him herself!

Available in July wherever paperback books are sold, or
through Harlequin Reader Service.

In the U.S.
901 Fuhrmann Blvd.
P.O. Box 1397
Buffalo, N.Y. 14240-1397

In Canada
P.O. Box 603
Fort Erie, Ontario
L2A 5X3

Take 4 best-selling love stories FREE
Plus get a FREE surprise gift!

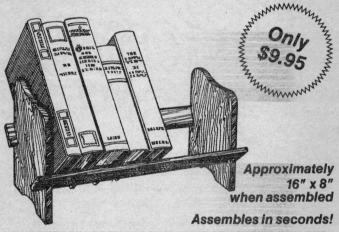